JIMMY PLUSH
TEDDY BEAR DETECTIVE

GARRETT COOK

Eraserhead Press
Portland, OR

ERASERHEAD PRESS
205 NE BRYANT
PORTLAND, OR 97211

WWW.ERASERHEADPRESS.COM

"Mr. Plush Detective" first published in Startling Adult Mysteries May 1951 edition
"Mr.Plush and the Dead Horse" first published in Strange Western Romance October 1951 edition
"Jimmy Plush and Mittens O' Hara in "Zuvembie Soiree"" first published in Reprobate Magazine February 1952
"Mr.Plush and the Chief Inspector" first published in Twofisted Suspenstories For Girls May 1953
"Jimmy Plush in the Tomb of the Martian Pharaoh" first published in Christian Boy's Adventure Digest vol. 6, April 1954

ISBN: 1-936383-63-2

Printed in the USA.

To Leza, to my mother, to Jeff Burk, Rose O'Keefe and Carlton Mellick. And to the 35 awesome individuals on the Plushlist...

It happened. The bear survived and so did I.
Thanks for doing what you did.

CONTENTS

Mr. Plush, Detective

Until a month ago, my name was Hatbox. Then, I woke up as a teddy bear in a trench coat and fedora. I wasn't just a teddy bear, I was worse; I was a teddy bear and a lowdown dirty private dick, the kind of gumshoe you hire when you want somebody found and don't care if somebody else has gotta get lost. From a hearty six one, I went down to three feet high, all because I needed money and Plush needed to be somebody else. When you got money, you can be anybody, which was lucky for the no-good, cuddly brown bastard that double crossed me. Next time a teddy bear offers to pay off your gambling debts in exchange for your body, you'd better think twice. I sure as hell should have.

Had I thought twice and not ended up as Jimmy Plush, I wouldn't have been sneaking into the warehouse where Lillian Benzedrine was being held. If I hadn't ended up as Jimmy Plush I wouldn't be padding around, palms frozen onto the oversized-trigger of a custom fingerless forty-five. Life is funny that way. Okay, so life is funny if you're the worst pulp writer on earth and don't have the foresight to think that life as a teddy bear would be perfectly peachy if I had my memories of my old life removed.

This was my eighth trip to warehouses like this in a month. Kidnappers are sloppy in this town. One look at the perpetrators said why. One of the two was a big guy, his face was clenched tight, his jaw square and he had a forehead you could serve a round of drinks for the house off. The other one looked like a ferret standin' on its hind legs, wore a long tie decorated with hearts. I knew them well by now, Halperin's men, Johnny Hideous and Skinny Valentine. Not much for brains or creativity, but I will admit that in the past they had been know to press their size advantage with some degree of effectiveness. In short, men who I'm embarrassed to say have literally knocked the stuffing out of me.

But, lucky for me, I've gotten used to this body (as much as a guy can get used to being a teddy bear the size of a toddler) and being tiny and made out of plush and stuffing makes you quiet. Quiet enough to sneak up behind a huge bruiser and shoot out the back of his knee at point blank range with a modified teddy bear .45. Mean enough to do it, too. If this warehouse had neighbors, Hideous definitely would've woken them up.

"Jimmy Plush, I'll teach ya! I'll teach ya to sneak up behind me!"

He was right. His falling to the floor writhing and screaming definitely taught me that I should sneak up on him. His partner reached for his gun, but I was quicker on the draw and shot him in the hand. Last time I'd encountered these two a week back, I was the one getting shot in the arm, while Hideous reached into me and started pulling cotton out. This was definitely a change for the better. Tangle with a couple of thugs nine times you start to figure things out.

Angry and bleeding, but not down for the count, Skinny charged me and though he wasn't the stronger of the two I was still a teddy bear. I realized now would be the time to make use of some of the Chinese fighting arts that my chauffeur Chang was training me in, fighting arts used by the real Jimmy Plush to put thugs like these in their places. The Angry Hamster Kick was perfected by vicious Shaolin dwarves for just these occasions, and sure enough, one good quick Hamster Kick used Valentine's momentum and size to cave his ribs in on themselves.

Since the two thugs would be more eager to get to a hospital than finish me off, I untied Mrs. Benzedrine and brought her out to the limo for delivery to her husband, who had tried to open a competing Chinese restaurant across the street from Vic Halperin's gaudy Chinese pleasure palace, J.L Wong's. Vic Halperin had never liked competition and David Benzedrine's mother was actually Chinese. As well as hating competition, Halperin hated the Chinese since his greatest desire in life was to be one of them. I pitied Benzedrine, since inheriting this body left me on Halperin's bad side from day one, and like him there was nothing I could do about what body I inhabited. Unlike him, I owned a gun and was training in the Chinese fighting arts. For a race of wisecracking chauffeurs and crooked restaurateurs, those Chinese sure know their fighting arts.

I proudly brought Mrs. Benzedrine to the door and rang the bell. Nothing. Knocked. Nothing. Something stank. I worked the knob and it turned out the door was open.

"I'll go in first, Mrs. Benzedrine. I think something's going on."

My chauffeur rolled down his window, perfect to the beat. It was uncanny how he did that all the time.

"Should Chang accompany most honored Mr. Plush inside?"

"Stay out here and wait."

"As you wish. But Chang is not sure…"

"Wait outside and be ready if I don't come out."

"Yes, Mr. Plush." Chang mumbled what must have been something rude in Chinese. I'll have to learn to speak slanty someday and take him by surprise. Someday.

Chang was right. Chang has an awful habit of being right. I opened the door, walked in to the sitting room and a walrus shot me in the chest. It was probably just a furry dressed as a walrus, but I still didn't expect to be shot in the chest by anything resembling a walrus. A squid, also definitely a furry, walked into the sitting room with a hand drill. Luckily, I black out from pain easily and am something of a fainter. Otherwise, I would have felt something nobody should ever feel.

When my eyes opened, I was disappointed but not surprised that the first thing I saw was the long, arrogant, wrinkly face of Vic Halperin, "the Pale Peril" as he's often called. The squinty eyes, the long, skinny fake moustache, the awful goatee, the cheap fez on his head. Halperin was no easier to look at than he was to talk to. He ran his press on nails over what I now understood to be a gaping hole in my stomach, proudly exploring its contours. I'm grateful that teddy bears don't bleed or vomit, because otherwise I'd be doing plenty of both things. He backed off, so I could look at the two Furries who knocked me out cold. And appreciate that Chang and the Benzedrines were all tied up beside me.

Chang's head was hanging.

"Chang apologizes to Honored Mr. Plush. There is no counter for squid style martial arts."

"That's alright, Chang," I said, mortified that all my stuffing was hanging out, "the cotton comes out of your next check."

Halperin cleared his throat and as expected, began a lengthy reprimand in his deep voice that was as far from being Chinese as he was, maybe more because it didn't have a cheap kimono and a fez to hide behind.

"Jimmy Plush, we meet again, detective, but this time, the advantage is of course my own. I'm sure that you were finally able to put Skinny Valentine and Johnny Hideous in the hospital, but as you can see, I have taken a higher class of thug, men who can't be outwitted by a two-bit stuffed bear who likes to stick his nose in the wrong honey pots."

It took a lot of willpower not to laugh. I restrained myself not out of any kind of fear of Halperin, but out of knowledge that laughing would make more of my stuffing start to fall out.

"How do you know it was me?"

"Mr. Plush, you have a very familiar face."

"Common too. You ever been to F.A.O Schwartz?"

Halperin liked to banter, but was always quick to get steamed. I wanted him to be off balance and give me some kind of advantage. It didn't work.

"That's very funny, Mr. Plush, but the fact is, something must be done about you."

"Give him to me," the walrus furry cooed, "he's so beautiful, so soft. I could have so much fun with him…"

The squid crossed his arms.

"I don't think he's so special." There was a hint of jealousy in his voice, but I didn't want to think about it.

"We could both have him, and it would be a delight."

"I suppose we could. He *is* beautiful."

"His fur has a lovely texture…"

Now I was starting to get afraid. Halperin was the kind of scum that would hand me over to his gunsels to have god-knows-what done to me. He also appreciated these guys more than he did Hideous and Valentine, even though they'd only been in his service a little bit. I hoped I could either get out of here before they did or lose enough stuffing to die so I wouldn't have to experience their plush flippers and tentacles on me.

"You see, Mr. Plush, what happens when you interfere with me? I'm sure you don't want Tusky and Bernstein to have their way with you, do you?"

"I must confess I would not." I tried to say it with my tough façade intact. I'm pretty sure I didn't pull it off quite right.

"So stay out of my way, or you'll be left to serve as a kind of toy which you were not intended to be."

"All right. I'll lay off your operation."

Halperin applauded softly.

"Excellent, Mr. Plush. Tusky, Bernstein, untie Plush and my countryman."

The walrus and squid complied.

"I hope to see you later," the walrus whispered in my ear. I hoped I never would.

I eased into my modified limo feeling like I'd been hit by a truck full of lightning being driven by my girl and the man she was making time with.

"Chang," I said to my chauffeur, "that was demoralizing."

"I cannot apologize enough, most honored Mr. Plush."

"Funny that you say that, Chang. *That* was just enough. Next time we go against Halperin, I hope there won't be any squids involved," I choked a little, "or walruses. God, I hope there aren't any walruses."

"The squid and walrus' success means there will be more of them. Maybe the time has come that for once you keep your word and leave Halperin alone."

I didn't like hearing that, especially coming from a Chinaman who was working for me. Chang had a tendency to say the wrong thing, particularly when it was the right thing. One of the few joys in my life of teddy bear detective inadequacy was messing with Halperin, especially since I had just gotten an innocent man and his wife killed for opening a Chinese restaurant on the wrong side of town. On the other hand, next time we squared off, I'd have to face Halperin's Furries. I didn't like losing and I didn't like admitting that I couldn't win. Chang had done something impressive: found a spot where I was even more vulnerable.

"It's your fault I got in this mess, Chang. Don't tell me whose cage I can rattle and whose I can't! This little bear's got teeth,

Chang and don't you forget it."

The argument ended abruptly when we both noticed the same thing: there were more furry girls on the streets. Usually they were rare and hard to pick up, but now there were squirrel girls or skunk girls or kitty cat girls or even killer whale girls peddling their wares everywhere. First Halperin employs Furries, now every pimp in the city must be doing it. Something didn't add up.

"You remember there being so many Furries in this town, Chang?"

"I can honestly say, Mr. Plush, that I do not. I have never seen two prostitutes dressed as turtles arguing over which lamppost to lean against in my life."

"Smells like Halperin."

Chang shot down my theory immediately.

"Mr. Halperin has been running the flesh trade in this city for years. Why would he just now put more furry girls on the streets, most honored Mr. Plush?"

"You've got a point Chang. Let's go to Jean's. There's nobody else I know who can patch me up and tell me about Furries in this town."

"A most wise suggestion, most honored Mr. Plush."

We drove to Jean's. She answered the door in her evening clothes, somehow having figured I'd come by. Her evening clothes happen to be a tight, head to toe fox suit. Somehow she pulls it off. I never bought into that Indian shamanic totem stuff, but that suit makes me wonder from time to time.

Being a teddy bear kind of blunts the impact of a near fatal wounding. Most guys show up with their guts hanging out, their girlfriend faints. Me? It's always the same:

"What have you done this time? Let me get my sewing box…"

"Your compassion moves me to tears."

"Your sarcasm bores me to tears. Come in and sit down on the bed."

So I did and she began to sew. As you can imagine, it hurt like hell, but not so bad as a gutshot does.

"You should really stop messing with Halperin."

And not as bad as a lecture either.

"The man's a crook and a bully. He deserves the trouble I give him."

Jean rubbed her nose against my forehead.

"But do you deserve the trouble he gives you, baby?"

Maybe if it wasn't for the fact that Halperin was Jean's employer I wouldn't be so scornful of him. Then again, it was money I owed him that made me sell my body to Jimmy Plush. It was between how he helped me end up as a teddy bear and how he was party to Jean leading her secret life of waitressing and crime and how he helped her make a fool out of me on account of it. I was no fool, but Halperin helped her think she could make a fool out of me and that was enough to make me hate him all over again for who he was. I might have actually started to like this girl if I could trust her – and I wanted to like her so much.

"No matter what happens to me, Vic Halperin gets no quarter."

"You shouldn't talk like that, Jimmy; Halperin's a big, dangerous man in this town!"

"And I'm a small, dangerous bear, Jean! I'm not gonna be scared of anybody, you hear me?"

Sure I meant it, sure the bravado was real, but it was still a bit much. Being three feet tall and having no penis makes a man want to overcompensate. Dripping cotton from a gaping chest wound makes a man angry. In the future I would have to remind myself that my tough guy private dick outburst count was getting to be a bit high.

"I've got to go."

I mustered the best sad teddy face I could. I was a pretty sad teddy.

"You sure?"

I was hoping this might go where it usually went when I was getting patched up. I lack equipment, but the Jean rubs me against all the right places and it feels nice. I could use a rub against all those places, because believe me, they could be oh so right and my day had gone oh so wrong.

"I've got things to do."

I knew what she meant. Waiting tables to help Halperin run

numbers, unloading crates of fake name brand cereal, plucking balls of opium so that the poor sods at the den hidden behind J.L Wong's were shortchanged. Things to do. Bad things to do. I was gonna find out what and break my word to Halperin as I always did, possibly getting the ever-loving shit beaten out of me like I usually did. Didn't matter. I was tired of this.

"Alright. Dinner Friday?"

"Maybe. I might be busy."

"Suit yourself. No fuzz off my balls. Thanks for the patch job."

"Any time."

"Yeah sure, any time."

I sulked my way out to the car and sat down.

"Chang…"

"Conceal the car, wait for Jean and follow her?"

"Yes, Chang. Do we do this that often?"

Chang didn't answer. He knew he was already on pretty thin ice thanks to the incident with Tusky and Bernstein. We waited and a car picked her up. It drove around in circles for awhile to avoid a tail, not knowing Chang's Chinese Shadow Driving skills would be more than enough to evade them. Shadow Driving was a recent addition to the Chinese Fighting Arts, but not an altogether unwelcome one. The car stopped and let her out. I didn't like what I saw.

Jean immediately began a brutal slap fight with a fat girl dressed like a squirrel for the use of her lamppost. In this city, a girl doesn't use a lamppost for reading light.

"So there you go, Chang," I boasted, "definitive proof."

"That your girlfriend is a prostitute?"

"I'm trying to objectively appraise the situation, Chang. Thinking about that too much will inhibit me. Jean works for Halperin, though. The Furries are on the street, one furry works for Halperin, therefore the Furries are Halperin's."

"I am still not convinced."

"Is there anybody else who might know something then, Chang?"

Chang's voice got more solemn than usual.

"Yes, most honored Mr. Plush, but he hates you."

"Doesn't everybody?" I didn't like the notion, but its veracity could hardly be disputed.

"Alright, Mr. Plush. Just don't expect him to cooperate much. Also, I must warn you, Mittens O' Hara, is unusual."

"Nothing's going to surprise me in this town."

Except that is for an office dominated by a large typewriter. And a fat tiger cat whose porkpie hat rested uncomfortably atop its fat head. There was a slip of paper that read "press" on it. The cat sat down on various keys to type out something in enormous letters. It was a surprise, though I've gotta say, I had thought Halperin was the last animal left in this town. As soon as it spotted me, it hissed.

"Beat it, Plush," said the cat in a high nasal New York huckster voice, "You know you isn't welcome here, not after what you did!"

"I'm afraid I don't know that I isn't welcome, Mittens. Otherwise I wouldn't be here."

"Well now you know, Paddington, so scram!"

I decided to ease up on the tough guy detective stuff for a second. This guy was every bit as abrasive as I was and there'd be no sense starting anything. My temper hadn't done me a whole hell of a lot of good lately.

"Listen, Mittens, I've got a big problem and I need your help. If you can't help me out this city's gonna get filthier and stay filthier. There's a rumor going around that somebody's helping Vic Halperin from the shadows. Somebody with furry connections. You don't want to mess with angry Furries and how long do you think it will be before you starting poking around and get caught by a better class of thug than Johnny Hideous and Skinny Valentine? Think about it, kitty cat!"

The cat did think about it, writing several lines of Qs as he sank down into his spot.

"As much as I, and anybody else in this town who's smart enough to count to three, I've gotta say, you have a point Plush. Guy like me gets into trouble all the time. Lots of tight squeezes, danger around every street corner. One day, Mr. Bartender starts slippin' fells gin with a knockout drop chaser and then, bang I'm on the trail and they're on my tail. Dangerous work, Plush. So,

I tell ya what, I'll give you the lowdown on the Furries in town, even though I don't like ya, and I want it to be known again, I don't like ya. You're a walking cold sore, Jimmy Plush and you make people regret ever knowin' ya. If I hadn't lost my body in a game of checkers with a cat, I'd have shot you by now, but I'm glad I didn't, because more Furries ain't good for anybody, more Furries always mean more trouble, don't they, Plush? So I'll tell ya, I'll…"

Bang!

The cat went silent and fell from his spot on the typewriter, reacting quickly, I reached for my gun, realizing somebody had come in while the cat was ranting, took aim and shot him and that somebody now had to be on the run. I could see the culprit running for the door, a guy in a penguin suit. Hopefully, all that padding wouldn't protect the back of his knees.

It didn't. He fell down right away, and it would be hard for him to get up. Particularly if I stood on his spine and pistol-whipped him in the back of his furry penguin head three or four times. Which I did. And he didn't get up. I ordered Chang inside and the two of us retrieved Mittens and the penguin thug. The thug went in the trunk and Mittens got the back seat next to him. Only difference was Mittens was going to the hospital and the penguin thug was definitely not.

"When you drop off Mittens, take me to Jean's, Chang."

"Certainly, most honored Jimmy Plush, but I don't think she'll be home."

"That's the point. She's got sewing needles and a bag of cotton."

Chang trembled a bit.

"You're starting to sound like the real Jimmy Plush."

"What was that?" the groggy, wounded Mittens mumbled, revealing that he might just pull through.

"I'll explain another day."

"Savin' my life almost makes up for what you did to me," said the cat, "almost."

So we brought the cat to the hospital. I couldn't stick around to find out if he'd pull through because I had some business with the guy who shot him. Some very unpleasant business. We dragged him into Jean's house and tied him to a chair in her kitchen. I climbed onto the counter and grabbed a sharp knife, while Chang peeled the penguin suit off the hood. Underneath it, he was even less to look at. I could see why he wanted so much to be cute.

His eyes opened to find me standing on the table brandishing a kitchen knife. I had also lain out the bag of cotton and Jean's sewing kit.

"I need some information," I said matter-of-factly.

"I don't know nothin'!"

"Aww, I wouldn't say that. You know how to shoot a cat. You also know that an orange beak is better than that ugly, scrunched up pug nose of yours. That's not nothin'. I know lots of people who know less than that."

The penguin thug spat at me.

"I'm not tellin' you nothin'!"

"See? There we go. Now we're communicating better. There's a difference between the two things."

"Yeah? What it is, bear?"

"If you don't know nothin', I could torture you all day and nothing would come out. But, if you just won't tell me anything than I could probably extract something."

The penguin thug coughed out a nervous fake laugh.

"Ha! That's rich comin' from the teddy bear. You ain't got the balls!"

I'm not certain if I had ever intended for this to be a bluff, but if I had, that possibility was gone now. As any man would be who lacked genitalia, I was awfully sensitive. I grabbed the knife with both hands and with all my teddy bear strength, I made a long cut in his bare chest.

"You Furries. You make me laugh. Walkin' around, pretending to be what I am. It's insulting. It's hilarious, too. I'm gonna give you what you want. Chang, stuff 'im."

My chauffeur's yellow skin turned pale.

"Mr. Plush…"

"Take the cotton and stick it in the hole, Chang. Then sew it."

The penguin thug's eyes widened. They must have looked enormous to Chang.

"Please, mister, you can't…"

Chang gave his customary bow.

"As you wish, most honored Mister Plush."

So, Chang stuffed the wound with cotton and sewed it shut. The penguin thug made several noises I never expected to hear out of a man or a penguin. I glared at him with my round, black plastic eyes. I knew he couldn't see any expression behind them, but from the look on his tear-stained face, I could tell that he knew I was glaring and he knew I wasn't above cutting him again.

"I do know somethin' and I'll tell ya."

"You don't say? I'm glad, because Chang could easily undo all those stitches one by one..."

"Halperin's working with a man from outta town who just started coming around. He knew this town was ripe for plucking. Halperin could be scared, could be shaken down. Halperin's a coward underneath the whole Mandarin act."

"Tell me something I don't know. And I mean that literally. Stop stalling. I am not a patient little bear."

"His name's Kewpie Doll Steve."

"Better. If he were in the phonebook, that is. Chang, undo the stitches."

Chang once more gave his customary bow. He elongated it, seeing that this time I actually was bluffing.

"Wait...you don't gotta do that. The Monogram Marshmallow factory's a front for his hideout."

Great. Kewpie Doll Steve was hanging out at the Monogram Marshmallow factory. The worst part of having lost my memory is having to rediscover what a stupid town I lived in one day at a time. There were towns where it was hard to solve a mystery, where it took a smart man and not a guy willing to torture idiot henchmen for answers. There were towns where furry prostitution wasn't a criminal calling. There were towns outside the protectorate of crotchety teddy bears. Somehow, I still felt attached to this one and it bugged the hell out of me.

I juggled my failures in my head like so many oranges; I had failed as a writer and failed as a gambler, so I failed as a person and traded bodies with Jimmy Plush, I had failed as a man not convincing my girl to get out of Halperin's press-on nailed grasp, I had failed as a detective when I got knocked out and left Lillian

Benzedrine to Halperin's very limited mercies. She was probably somewhere dressed up as a French poodle to amuse out-of-town businessmen as her husband dangled in a chair over a vat of acid. My conscience was in the same position and there were scissors at the rope. Snip. Splash. Stab. I plunged the knife deep, penetrating his heart as all the disappointments had mine.

I waited for Chang's reaction. I wanted him to shake his head in disappointment. I wanted him to cry or tell me I'd gone too far and he should've been spared since he gave me the information he needed. But Chang had worked for the real Jimmy Plush, who had done things Chang refused to tell me about, who had done things that made Chang grateful for me, as bitter as I could get and as sick as could I be of his small outbursts of impertinence in the midst of fawning loyalty. Chang wasn't surprised.

"Your orders, Mister Plush?"

I sighed.

"Finish the job, Chang. We need to send a message; we need Halperin to know that Jimmy Plush is no fool, no weakling and isn't going to be pushed around."

So Chang and I got to it. It took hours, stank like nothin' else I've ever smelled and we had to buy a lot more cotton and give Jean's kitchen quite the scrubbing, but it was worth it. Halperin would get the message now, and I wouldn't have to do this again. Hopefully. I can't say I was that crazy about the whole experience. We dropped off the corpse outside J.L Wong's and drove like the wind for the Monogram Marshmallow factory, where Kewpie Doll Steve or somebody who knew where he was should have been.

I can't say I was at all shocked to find "Halperin's" gunsels Tusky and Bernstein guarding the back door. Might be a big city, but it was a pretty damn small world. Much as I wanted a piece of that walrus, stuffing that penguin had slightly eased my thirst for revenge, and I was thinking clearer.

"Chang, you take down the walrus, I'll take the squid."

Chang was concerned.

"You realize there is no counter to squid style martial arts."

"I do, Chang."

"And you are angry at the walrus…"

"Don't worry about me, Chang. I'm sure it will all work out."

I sprang from the car and put a bullet right between Bernstein's eyes. There was no counter to squid style martial arts, but as of yet the Chinese really hadn't come up with a way to get around being shot in the head. Having untied the Gordian Knot with my gun, Chang readied himself for the walrus' charge. Tusky could have countered the Chinese fighting arts as well, but was, as I suspected, blinded with grief and anger at the death of his lover.

Poor Tusky charged directly into a move whose name Chang says translates roughly into "Gilded Battle Axe Fist". The walrus vomited out a big fishy mess and then imploded. Made me wonder why Chang had never chosen to do that before. It would have made things much easier.

Of course, it wasn't *that* easy. The ruckus of the exploding walrus and the vanquished squid attracted some attention. Plenty of attention. The door burst open and there were all manner of Furries on the other side of it, from neon yellow opossums, to perpetually smiling wolves, from angry rats to loveable mandrills to cartoonish chipmunks to placid, Zen tortoises. There were some fifty of them pouring out of there, but we were ready to make some fur fly.

High on our victory, we took them three, four at a time; me letting bullets fly, tripping up a pink cow with a low kick as I shot a badger in the eye. With the Gilded Battle Axe Fist and the Decapitation Kick, Chang went through a pair of cuddly coyotes without blinking an eye and then brought the fear of God into a young tortoise that fled surprisingly fast. I took a few punches, dodged a few bullets, but I gave better than I got, because I'm Jimmy Plush and there ain't no walking stuffed animal in this town, real or fake that can stand up to me when I'm angry and I've just put a bullet in the head of somebody who I thought was unbeatable. Plush heads and the real heads underneath them littered the alley outside the Monogram Marshmallow Factory. There's nothing like the scent of fake fur, hot lead and spilled guts in the night to prove you're a real man.

"Chang, you've redeemed yourself," I said to the chauffeur, "but I need you to stay in the car."

"Mr. Plush, who knows what kind of ambush…"

"I think the ambush is over. I'm going in to investigate and hopefully find Kewpie Doll Steve."

"As you wish, most honored Mr. Plush."

Like I said, in some towns mysteries are tough to solve and it takes a real smart man to unravel it all but this ain't one of the towns. Criminals, God bless 'em, were usually found exactly where you expected to find them, completely unafraid of being undermined by the likes of myself or the frequently absent police department. Emerging from the shadows, walking past two large inflatable sculptures of Murray, the Monogram Unicorn was a figure about my size.

As he stepped into the light, I saw how eerily Kewpie Doll Steve looked like a she. Like my own empty plastic eyes, his showed no feeling, but looked a bit flirty on account of the long, curled eyelashes and nonexistent eyebrows. His huge, infant lips had been painted red, which was the color of the short, checkered dress he wore. The ensemble was completed by a pair of little white party shoes. The illusion broke when he laughed a heavy cigar-burned laugh.

"This is him? The guy who brought down my men? Who gives Vic Halperin trouble? You're a riot, Jimmy Plush. You're just as much of a joke as me!"

I squeezed off a shot at the doll, but now of all times, the gun clicked "sorry, out of ammo".

"Don't worry, Plush. I don't have a gun. Don't need one either, teddy bear!"

The talking doll was quick and caught me off guard, he leapt like a jaguar, pinning me to the ground and punching me hard in the face. A guy like this was strong for the same reason I had to be strong: cause he looked nothing like a man. Cause he looked soft. As the punches rained down like brokers when the market goes south, I understood more than ever why I was so angry. I rolled him off me and took his position on top.

His head squeaked with each of my blows, which left me wondering just what could be done to a guy like this. Could he be brain damaged? Could he be unstuffed? Not by a guy with no hands who doesn't have anything to cut him with. I was out of bullets, too. I'd have to do something the criminals in this town usually didn't require me to do and that was think. I got off him and danced around like a boxer, putting up my knuckleless dukes.

Kewpie Doll Steve kicked surprisingly hard again, sending me flying backwards into the side of a marshmallow vat. It was hot. I moved away from it quickly, knowing my own flammability a bit too well thanks to a run-in with Skinny Valentine and a cigarette lighter a few weeks back. I scurried lightly up the ladder leading up to the vat, hoping Kewpie Doll Steve might be dumb enough to follow. Naturally, he took the bait.

I scrambled up the ladder one step at a time, defending my position with punch after punch and from punch after punch. Every couple of hits, I would be nearly as oblivious as he was or lose my footing on the ladder, but then the plan would come back to me, along with the knowledge that there would be no other way to bring this guy down. Pathetic that I had to rely on a vat of hot marshmallows.

We reached the top and I shuffled along the rim, balance aided by my relative lack of mass, his balance aided by the same. I risked my position to rush him and nearly fell in myself. Like Holmes and Moriarty, we were caught up in a moment of mortal struggle and almost plunged to the death together. Almost. My hands found the rim as he fell screaming into the white, hot gooey abyss. Awful way to go. I shuffled along the rim again until I reached the ladder and worked my way down to enjoy my moment of triumph.

I should have known I was never that lucky. When I hit the ground, a bullet caught me in the back, bringing me down. I felt my consciousness start to puff out of my body like a wisp of smoke. I wish I wasn't a guy who fainted so easily. The trenchcoated assassin left his hiding place and climbed gracefully up the ladder, reaching in, grabbing the marshmallow covered Kewpie Doll Steve from the pit of ooze and climbing down just as quickly as he climbed up. Before blacking out completely I caught a glimpse of the guy's face. Just when I thought my day had gotten better, it went back to being a regular god-awful day in the life of Jimmy Plush, teddy bear detective. The face had been my own only a month back, the face of one Charles Hatbox, but behind the eyes there was the bear with whom I'd traded bodies, that bastard, the real Jimmy Plush.

Mr. Plush and
the Dead Horse

Being a gumshoe is stressful. Being a gumshoe in the body of a three foot teddy bear is a hell of a lot more stressful than that. So I decided to take the day off for once. Since trading my body to that teddy bear bastard to pay off my gambling debts, the closest thing I'd gotten to time off was time spent face down in an alley unconscious. And unlike some people, I wasn't there for leisure. I knew this day would start off with a couple of annoyances, but I thought it would end at that. The first one, I'd figured on. Having no private residence, I had a tendency to sleep in my office. I also had a lapdog of a Chinese chauffeur that had a habit of waiting outside with my limo ready to go and a tragic attempt at coffee in his hand. I stepped outside, and I was right. There was Chang with coffee staler than politics and pictures. I sighed.

"Chang, where do they grow the coffee in China?"

Even for a Chinaman, Chang went stiff.

"They do not grow coffee in China, Most Honored Mister Plush."

I took the coffee from him. This was an important part of my morning ritual lately.

"Do you wanna know why they don't grow coffee in China, Chang?"

He sighed. There was anger behind his slanty subhuman eyes.

"Yes, Mister Plush. I would like to know why."

I tossed the coffee in his face as I did every morning. The coffee was piping hot. Good old Chang. Even confronted with certain scalding he wouldn't serve me lukewarm coffee.

"That is the worst damn coffee I've ever had. You run somebody's laundry through the pot?"

Chang folded his hands and bowed.

"Humblest apologies. Does Most Honored Mister Plush require breakfast? Or to be driven somewhere?"

"Does sycophantic Chang want to lose his job and have to

make noodles for a living?" It's important to be firm with one's chauffeur.

"Chang is very sorry." He bowed again. Chang bowed pretty often. Unavoidable when a kid hears Confucius in the nursery.

"I'm taking the day off, Chang."

Chang looked at me as if I were the one that talked goofy all the time.

"Are you certain Mister Plush, there is a lot to be done, there is especially the matter of…"

I didn't even wanna think about it.

"It can wait. He'll wait."

Chang laughed. "I do not think I would take getting shot as lightly as you have."

"I don't take it lightly, Chang. I got no leads, and I'm burnt out, so scram!"

Chang shrugged, got in the limo and drove off.

This left me alone. I called Jean and invited her to dinner. She said seven. I said not to wear the suit. She said I could go to Hell. I asked if she had any messages for her mother. She asked about the mess in her kitchen. I said I'd see her at seven and hung up, taking my phone off the hook afterwards. Within five minutes, I started pouring myself drinks. I was bored to tears.

There was a knock on the door. Chang was starting to make me real angry. How could people with so much opium in their country be so utterly against relaxation? I opened my door, wishing the chinaman had made me two cups of coffee. I wouldn't drink the second one either. But it wasn't Chang at the door. It was a pony wearing a police cap. There was a whistle and a badge around his neck. It seemed like the sort of thing that would be a bad omen. What did my granny from the old country say about a pony on your doorstep? Made me wish I hadn't given up my memories during the transfer so I'd know things like that, like if I had a granny or where the hell the old country was.

"Sorry, pal," I said to the pony, "this ain't a stable and I'm closed for the day."

"Listen, Plush," the pony shot back in a voice that reminded me a little of Gary Cooper, "you don't like me and I don't like you, but I've got a problem. I'm gonna set aside my prejudices so we can make this town a little less awful."

"Not interested. Go find yourself some oats and leave me alone, Seabiscuit."

The pony got in my face.

"I don't think you understand. I've got three dead city councilmen and a dead socialite. Think about it, four prospective kidnap victims. If they keep bumping off these people, there will be nobody to kidnap and murder's one per customer, Plush. How long do you think a shameless shamus like yourself's gonna last in a city where all the victims are already dead?"

He had a point. If I was going to maintain this lifestyle, I couldn't have somebody icing every client that could pay me. Maybe I didn't want to maintain this lifestyle, but when you're a teddy bear with a bad reputation and nothing going for you but a chauffeur and office with "Jimmy Plush, Detective" on the door and a custom teddy bear handgun there usually ain't many career paths open for you.

"Okay, horsey, you've got my attention. Now give me the details. Come on in."

But before he could, three shots rang out and he was good as glue. If a pony on my doorstep was a bad omen (and I couldn't really tell if it was), then a dead pony on my doorstep was an awful one and a dead pony on my doorstep that had a badge was a disaster. I had to sort this out and I needed to do it fast.

Lucky for me, Chang had not really taken off, but had instead parked the limo in an alley nearby and waited for me to change my mind. He pulled up to the curb, got out and gave me a bow. Even though I needed him now, I was not happy about this.

"I guess they don't have days off in China either, huh?"

Chang smiled.

"And yet, I'm not the one with a dead policeman on my doorstep."

"Who is he? He knew the real Plush and hated him. Must have been a pretty good egg. For a pony."

Chang's smile turned into a frown.

"He was. His name was Horskowitz. He was an honest cop, not into the same things the others are. He tried to put some of them away for corruption, so they beat him up, transferred him into the body of a pony. He didn't quit. He felt that only showed how much he was needed. In my opinion, he was right."

I could only think of one man that could be behind this.

"Chang, take me to J.L Wong's."

The scenery on the way to J.L Wong's was pretty much the same tableau of heartbreak I was used to; Furries in species drag ranging from strap-on sporting mice to Murray the Monogram Unicorn waiting for clients against every lamppost, ugly hoods carrying violin cases, businessmen looking for a den where they could chase the dragon, a Chinatown that the Orientals were afraid to even go near. Same hell-on-earth where most of my cases ended up leading. Or was it? There was a giant black cloth tent covering the side of the street. Something huge was underneath, something the size of a few buildings or a gigantic warehouse. I hadn't seen any construction or demolition going on last time I was here, and last time I was here was two days ago. Identical obese quintuplets in pink pinstripe suits stood outside guarding it. They were trying too hard to act natural.

"Chang, stop!" By the time I'd said it, he'd already stopped.

I got out since I had a sneaking suspicion that these five gentlemen might have had something to do with my case.

"Nice weather we're havin', huh?"

"Yes," they said in unison.

"So…gentlemen, what's under the cloth?"

"A carnival," they replied, again in unison.

"It'll never work," I told them as I walked back to the car to shake down the notorious proprietor of J.L Wong's, "this town's already too much fun."

I returned to the limo.

"Did they tell you what was under the cloth?"

"They said it was a carnival."

Chang shook his head.

"There is much to fear from men who do not need to try."

"You shouldn't be so cynical, Chang. What's the matter? Don't like cotton candy?"

We shared an uncomfortable laugh. I kept the shudder that followed to myself. A carnival doesn't usually make heavy breathing sounds.

"Still going to J.L Wong's then?"

"Wouldn't want Vic to get lonely."

Chang parked outside of J.L Wong's. I would've thought that as often as I'd come to this place, I'd be used to the blinding glare of neon outside and the dinginess. In fact, it wasn't just dingy, this place was dark as a panther's asshole lit only by a tiny, swinging paper lantern over each table and the glint of golden dragons on the wall. You couldn't even see the smiling face of the Buddha on the stage where a bleach blonde floozy butchered "They Can't Take That Away From Me" every day. I sat down and waited to be served. A waitress in a crocodile suit blew me a kiss but didn't come to take my order. I knew full well who would have that privilege.

The anvil headed man mountain known as Johnny Hideous and the human pencil Skinny Valentine approached the table.

"You were warned, Plush," said Hideous, "seems like you don't like keeping your stuffing on the inside."

I yawned.

"So, out back, gentlemen?"

Skinny Valentine laughed.

"Boy, Plush, you sure are stupid. You've earned the biggest pounding you've ever gotten. We might just rip you apart at the seams, toss you in a garbage bag and make sure nobody puts you together."

I got serious.

"The reason I ask, boys, is because I'm in a hurry. I got dinner at seven and a dead cop on my doorstep. I don't have time to pencil in "shoot to wound". So, I'd like for you gentlemen to take me to your boss."

They whispered among themselves. As they did so, I drew my custom teddy bear .45.

"Well? I ain't got all day."

Johnny Hideous was starting to sweat.

"Sure, Plush, we'll let the Pale Peril decide what to do with you."

So I was led in to Halperin's office. The place was too large for anyone to do business, there was practically a hallway between the door and his desk, which was a plank of wood set on top of a stuffed tiger. There was a gigantic gong at his back, engraved with the image of him making violent love to that very tiger. Halperin was himself dressed as gaudy as he tended to, though he'd added a few inches to his giant fake goatee and the makeup around his eyes to make 'em look slanty was thicker than ever. Something real unsavory about a man that gets more oriental every time you see him.

"Ah, Mister Plush. It's been a couple days. I should have known you'd come around sometime soon."

"You killed a horse, Halperin. And this time I don't think it was to make your chow mein."

Halperin motioned for Skinny and Johnny to come closer. They whispered among themselves. Johnny and Skinny did a lot of shrugging. For some reason Skinny was using his hands to illustrate the size of something gigantic. Hideous shook his head. Halperin sent them away. Away from the room altogether.

"Plush," said Halperin with a sigh, "I'm worried for you. As an oriental criminal supergenius, I need my archnemesis to be on his toes and you've come in here babbling about a horse that I didn't even kill."

This was getting interesting. Not that Halperin was starting to pity me, but that he clearly had no idea what I was talking about. I decided I would keep on him, though because maybe he would help lead me to somebody who did.

"Don't play dumb with me, Vic. You know who killed Horskowitz."

The Pale Peril got a little bit paler.

"Horskowitz? The cop?"

"No, Horskowitz the Wonder Dog. What do you think?"

"I think the last honest cop in this town is dead. Part of me wishes I'd done it myself, but part of me…"

I laughed and took a swig from the bottle of gin in my pocket.

"Lot of bigger fish in this town than you. Kewpie Doll Steve using you as his errand boy and now whoever paid for this hired gun could cut in on your territory."

I walked to Halperin's desk, jumped up so I could set down the bottle of gin.

"I think you need this more than I do."

I wish the gesture hadn't been so exhausting and difficult. It would have been a lot more dramatic. I left, returning to the car empty-handed.

"Wasn't Halperin."

I had barely gotten into the limo before Chang said this.

"You could've told me before I wasted my time in that cut-rate chink cathouse. How'd you know?"

"Skinny Valentine and Johnny Hideous would have stayed to mess you up. If it were some of the muscle from Kewpie Doll Steve, then you'd have been able to see them making their escape. Furries can kill, but they don't run so well."

I sighed. Halperin didn't need the gin more than I did.

"If you're so smart, tell me how we can flush him out."

"Well," Chang replied, his voice oozing with confidence, "one surefire way is to run a Chinese man for mayor."

The confidence oozed away.

"Uh oh."

"To City Hall, Chang."

"Most honored, Mr. Plush…"

"Sorry, Chang, I have to flush this guy out."

Chang mumbled something in Chinese. I suspected it was derogatory, so noted to myself I would have to find another chance to scald Chang with hot coffee. Or maybe soup.

The lines in City Hall almost extended out the door. I didn't have time for this, so I figured I'd trade on my bad reputation and do the sort of thing that would be expected of a dangerous heel like Jimmy Plush.

"I'm Jimmy Plush! I'm Jimmy Plush!" I screamed as I fired my gun at the ceiling. I only needed to do this for about ten seconds before I was at the front of the line and Chang was registered to run for mayor. Podiums were set up outside for a debate within five minutes. Since the existing mayor still had three and a half years in his term, only one other candidate had registered to run; a chronically incontinent Furry who had not changed his excrement stained giraffe suit for years. Still, I think Chang wouldn't have had a shot in hell.

Luckily, I didn't need Chang to have a shot, I needed him to *get* shot and sure enough, five seconds after he stepped up to the podium, he had to dodge a bullet flying at his head. He did so easily, expert at the fighting and dodging arts that he was. When the assassin took his second shot, I observed the angle he'd been shooting from and discerned that he had to be shooting from a nearby alley, taking cover behind some trashcans. Using a Chinese flying bat kick that Chang had taught me, I managed to leap off the podium and into the trashcans, kicking one of them over.

When the trashcan dropped, I noticed that there was not an assassin, but a gun floating in the air. Surely, this had to be an invisible man. This invisible man shot me in the gut, then took off running. I took aim and shot him in the back. The bullet went right through him. Damn. Intangible and invisible. At least that's what I thought. He turned around.

"What the hell was that supposed to be?" said a tiny voice. It was coming from the gun.

"You tried to shoot my chauffeur so I shot you in the back."

The gun let out a tiny sigh.

"And you thought I was an invisible man? Invisible criminals are a dime a dozen, but me? I'm so much better."

He shot me again. I wasn't fast enough to dodge bullets like Chang could, but I was quick enough to put out my shoulder so I wouldn't take it in the head.

"That all you got?" I was losing a lot of stuffing, but I knew how I could put this guy through a lot worse than I was going through.

"Ha!" the gun snorted, "I'm the deadliest man on earth! All I could do in life was to kill, so I had my psyche implanted in this gun. I'm the perfect murderer! I don't have to sleep or eat, I have no biological urges but to shoot!"

"Yeah, well, you've only got three shots left to kill me."

He fired again. I held out my hand and took it there. Four shots. He aimed for my head next. It caught me in the ear.

"Goddamn slippery little bear!"

"Only two shots left," I gloated, "you're gonna have to bring me down quick."

He laughed.

"I'm not falling for that trick."

"Who's trying to trick you? I'm telling you, you have two shots left."

"You think I'm pretty dumb, don't ya?"

I did. I think most people are pretty dumb. Because they are.

30

Especially when a man becomes nothing but an itchy trigger finger. The thing about weapons is that anybody can set them off. That had to get to a guy. A man gets a gun because he wants freedom, the freedom to wave it around, lording it over his fellow man, the freedom to give and take life with impunity. I inched toward him.

"All this time you didn't realize that anybody could pick you up, point you in any direction and squeeze all the life out of your magazine?"

The gun trembled. He saw there was some truth in what I said. And he was off balance. Just where I wanted him.

"You stand back, bear! You move again and I'll…"

I laughed. It hurt to laugh, but I needed the edge.

"You'll what? You'll fire off your last bullet to stop me from firing off your last bullet?"

The gun spun around in midair indecisively. It knew I had a point. It also knew I'd been trying to bluff it. I took another step closer.

"I'm warning you! Not another step! I don't believe you! You're trying to fool me! I'll kill you!"

I came closer. Another step and I'd be an arm's length away, and that meant getting my hands on it, and that meant an end to the freedom the brute had taken on this form to get. He wouldn't let that happen.

"Stay back!" the gun screamed one last time. I didn't. I took the step, I reached. It shot me in the gut. Almost point blank. Stuffing everywhere. Had a feeling I was close to dead. Knew the gun wasn't as lucky. It wasn't. It lay on the ground lifeless, empty, without purpose.

Hearing no more sounds of commotion, Chang came running to find the gun and I. He picked me up, draped me over his shoulder.

"Chang…" I said feebly, "get the gun."

He put me in the car. Put the gun in the glove box. Looked at me with deep concern in his slanty little eyes.

"I know I should have brought the sewing kit! You're almost dead!"

I shook my head.

"No, Chang. Dead is when you run out of ammo."

Jimmy Plush and Mittens O'Hara in Zuvembie Soiree

So, I'm driving back to the office, chest riddled with bullets and all of a sudden, there's a loud thud and the limo begins to shake. Chang stopped the car, got out and let out the sort of shriek you'd expect from a debutante who found a negro in her bushes. He jumped up and down, scurrying like a squirrel on hot coals. Naturally, I can't help but check out what's goin' on. The Chinese are by nature a cowardly people, but Chang has an iron will most of the time. What the hell could this be about? I didn't mind losing a little stuffing to investigate the scene.

We should've kept driving. The kid was already pretty dead, crushed by the limo and merged with bits of the bicycle he was riding. It was no use checking out the corpse and there's nothing that can be done for a ten year old bicycle messenger hit by a speeding limousine. I didn't believe this when it happened. I'm made of Plush and stuffing, not stone. I'm not a bad enough guy to have thought at the time of an accident that we should drive over a child's corpse and keep going. I'm saying that now because I know what became of this particular car accident, I think it would have been better if we kept driving, or at least if we hadn't read the note in the kid's pocket.

But, I did read it. And I couldn't believe it.

"Good god, Chang, does anybody else in this town get mail?"

Chang shrugged.

"We WERE on the way to your office. It almost stands to reason that somebody would be carrying a letter for you."

"We should've kept going. I've got a date."

Chang laughed. He had good reason to laugh.

"I know, she'll probably cancel."

I went back to the note.

"There is a soiree tonight at the mayor's mansion," it read, "and something strange is going on. We must investigate. You owe me big, Plush. Your "friend" Mittens O' Hara. P.S the booze is free and there's a big client in it for you."

Hmm. Big client. Free booze. Worse had happened to me lately. A poor kid had died to get me the message from that damn cat so the least I could do was attend.

"I don't think you should go," said Chang, who had of course been reading over my shoulder (being only three feet tall, that's not hard for people to do). There was a degree of nervousness beating out his typical Confucian chill.

"And why do you say that?"

"You have a date, most honored Mr. Plush."

"A date you laughed off a few seconds ago, Chang."

"I like to laugh."

"No, you don't. You're Chinese."

"Ah so…" he replied.

It didn't take a detective to deduce that something was wrong with my Chinaman.

"Is there a reason you don't want to go to the mayor's house, Chang?"

"Yes."

"Will you tell me this reason?"

"Yes."

He did not respond for several seconds. So, I tapped my foot impatiently. He still did not respond.

"Well?"

"I can't tell you."

"You just said you could."

"The wise man bends like the supple reed."

"And the wiseass breaks like the fragile twig."

"Ah so…"

"What does that even mean?"

"I don't know. I don't speak Japanese. But we can look it up back at the office while you get ready for your date with Jean."

This was a little more than I could take.

"Chang, I'm angry, wounded and not naturally a patient little bear. What is wrong with you?"

"Don't be so hard on yourself."

"Chang!"

The Chinaman hanged his head.

"They say there are spirits in the mayor's home."

"I know, that's why I'm going. I could use some free booze after getting shot so much."

Chang remained stone-faced. It conflicted a lot with the mood of this quirky vaudevillian interlude.

"Spirits of the dead. Strange ghosts."

"Come on, Chang, aren't you just a little too old to be scared of ghosts?"

Chang shook his head defiantly.

"No sir, Mister Plush. Those ghosts are over a century old and I'm sure *they* know they're scary."

"Chang, when we get back to the office, make sure to brew me a pot of coffee."

He did, even knowing that I wanted nothing more from it than to splash it in his face. He cleaned the coffee off his face, stitched me up a little and we looked around for a tuxedo. Turns out I didn't even own a pair of pants. Looks like I'd have to make sure nobody took my coat. With all these preparations complete, Chang started to drove me to the mayor's house.

The mayor's house was made of elephant ivory and surrounded by the graves of Nero City's most prominent citizens. It was easy to see what left my primitive chauffeur's once neatly bound feet quaking in his boots.

"Chang shall wait in car."

"I won't have it, Chang. Without my chauffeur, how am I supposed to look important? You're going in with me. The only spooks here are washing dishes in the kitchen."

"I don't know about that, Mister Plush…"

"You don't know about much of anything, Chang, you're the chauffeur and I'm the boss. The chauffeur does what the boss tells him to."

"Well, if I get killed by ghosts, consider it my resignation."

"No, but I'll dock your pay for your funeral."

"You've done worse."

We went to the door and rang the bell. I expected some big, mute negro to answer so imagine my surprise at seeing a shapely dame in a fox suit, one whose curves I knew all too well. We exchanged hellos that might as well have been business cards. She offered to take my coat and hat. Neither of us laughed. I had a hard time remembering what had made me love this woman and I was sure at this point she had a hard time remembering what had made her love me. It doesn't stop me from loving her and I wonder if it doesn't stop her. She said nothing else to me until she announced me to the party, a room full of dull socialites who would have had to try pretty hard to manage to contribute less to society.

"Jimmy Plush, Teddy Bear Detective." She was not enthusiastic about saying it and the socialites were not enthusiastic about hearing it. A fat lady in pearls actually fainted. While she was on the ground, a little guy in a big coat with blonde curly hair and a funny nose mounted her and started raping her unconscious body, honking a horn the whole time. This caused another fat lady in pearls to faint dead away. An Italian organ grinder grabbed the necklace off her neck and made a run for the door. I tripped him, kicked him in the head until he was out cold and returned it, hoping to get some kind of reaction. More polite applause. Bastards.

The doorbell rang again and Jean ran off to get it. She returned with a cat in a tuxedo and a ravishing blonde. You know the type. Leggier than a millipede convention, with enough up top to fill a sweater and a half.

"Mittens O' Hara of the Nero City gazette and Miss Kate Hall."

Mittens and the dame don't bother to mingle. They approach me right away.

"Glad to see you got my message," says Mittens.

"No, actually, my limo got your messenger. Who is this ravishing beauty with you, pussycat?"

"This ravishing beauty is the mayor's daughter," the cat reporter shoots back, "and you've got about as much of a chance with her as you do of getting a Nobel Prize or the World's Tallest Man record."

"There's no reason to be rude, Mr. O' Hara," says the blonde icily.

"Sorry, kid. The bear and I go back a long way and I wish he'd go back to wherever he came from."

"This is no time for jokes, Mr. O' Hara. We have called upon the famous Mister Plush and one only calls upon the famous Mister Plush in the most dire of circumstances."

"I wouldn't say that, toots. You can call upon me in all kinds of circumstances."

She raised an eyebrow. In disgust.

"I prefer my men…bigger."

"I'll stand on a chair."

She started to cry.

"Mister Plush, my father, he's been acting so strange…"

"What happened? Did he turn into a Democrat?"

The conversation was cut off when I heard Jean announce another couple guests.

"Johnny Hideous and Skinny Valentine, respectable tradesmen!"

My frequent sparring partners had for some reason been invited to this soiree. I took note of this as it was both suspicious and dumb. They had traded their cheap suits for matching red tuxedos, which only served to remind me that Johnny Hideous' shoulders would serve the world better as a bookshelf and that Skinny Valentine should seek employment as the world's first homosexual scarecrow. Hideous wasted no time making an impression on the hoity-toities. He grabbed the blonde curly haired fella from off the society matron he was humping and tossed him against the wall so hard that his head cracked open, making a distasteful brain and bone stain. There was wild applause for this. A few of the society gentlemen exchanged business cards with him. There was a round of "For He's a Jolly Good Fellow". Bastards.

Kate Hall loudly cleared her throat. I turned back around, feeling like a real schmuck for giving Johnny Hideous my attention when I could have been looking at those gams and that chest. Perhaps Jean was right in her accusations that I spent too much time thinking about the people I wanted to kill. What Jean didn't understand was that my enemies had a leg up on her in that if they did something to make me mad, I could shoot them.

"Sorry, doll. Got distracted."

"See that it doesn't happen again." Her tone was almost impossibly stern.

"I can't make any promises unless you put a sweater on over that dress. Then again, if it's the right sweater, you could be even more distracting."

"This is hardly the time for flirting, Mister Plush. My father has been acting very strangely. He spends his days drooling, nodding his head and signing any document he's given."

"I'm no Sigmund Freud, lady, but my diagnosis is that your father's a politician."

Mittens rolled his eyes and walked away to investigate the party a little closer. And by the party I mean a platter of herring. Kate put her hands on her hips in annoyance.

"Mister Plush, it is time to get serious."

"All right, but I think this relationship is moving a little fast."

I got down on one knee.

"So how 'bout it, will you marry me?"

She gasped.

"I don't know, this is so sudden, but…yes."

"There. Case closed. Now let's find your father and get his blessing."

"My father's a drooling idiot."

"Then it should be pretty easy."

Kate's pretty blue eyes teared up again.

"Mister Plush, you must find out what happened to him. If we are to proceed with our wedding, I must have that peace of mind."

She needed peace of mind and I needed a piece of her so from the looks of things I was gonna have to do the job I came here to do. Whatever that was. But before I could do that, there was of course, another interruption.

It was a tap on the shoulder from behind. I turned, expecting one of my many enemies, but instead saw Jean.

"Mister Plush, you and I have business in the coatroom."

"Sorry, sweetheart, I don't think we do. I'm engaged to be married."

"No you're not."

"Unhand my fiancée, you floozy!" Kate screamed at her.

Jean sighed loudly.

"Look, it's not about that."

"So why would I be interested?" I retorted.

"Please, Mister Plush, this is very important."

So I followed her to the coat room and she showed me something I didn't see very often; her face. She took off the head of her fox suit and looked me in the eyes. I wish I'd gotten to see her eyes more often, because they were gorgeous, emerald green. This time they were filled with terror.

"I want you to know that I am not here of my own volition. I do not want to be apart from you. I love you, Jimmy Plush."

She put the fox head back on as if to say there was no more time for anything. I didn't like it because what she just said was the sort of thing she'd only say to me if she thought that she was never going to see me again. I should have told her that I loved her, I loved her even though she was crooked and a whore and a Furry. Sometimes a man forgets things like that. I exited the coatroom more sad and confused than when I entered it.

But the confusion and sadness gave way to anger pretty quickly. A top-hatted man, handsome save for his beady eyes and biggish nose slapped my fiancée. He immediately struck me as something of a shady character since the Italian jewel thief was standing beside him wearing a blank, vacant expression and a well pressed new tuxedo. I prepared to rush the top-hatted man from behind for hittin' my girl but the Italian jewel thief saw me coming and held out his leg to trip me, which had a series of consequences, the least of which was me falling. Chang, who had been standing in the corner to avoid trouble saw me hit the floor and fainted. I fainted a lot, but I'd never seen Chang do it. This party was no good for the Chinaman's usually indomitable nerves. Luckily for Chang, Mittens got his fat face out of the herring and decided to help Chang out, licking his face with his sandpapery tongue until he came to. Unluckily for Chang, his faint drew the attention of a nearby rich so-and-so, a white-haired, mustachioed man, who, while deciding that pants might not be appropriate for the occasion still sported a pith helmet and monocle.

"I say," he said, "isn't that the Chinaman that recently ran for mayor?"

Chang was smart enough to duck as soon as he heard the words "Chinaman" and "mayor" in the same sentence. More bullets, knives, throwing stars and blow darts than I'd ever seen in one place embedded themselves in the wall behind him. A group of cloaked figures heretofore unnoticeable made a mad dash for the door, their locations and agendas revealed. At least they didn't decide to stick around and try to do the job right. I got up off the floor, feeling more than a little perturbed by this party.

"Hey!" I shout at the top-hatted man, "what are you doin' hittin' my girl?"

The top-hatted man gasped in shock, then pulled a sheet of paper out of his pocket.

"Your girl? I'm afraid not, sir. I have here a marriage certificate signed by the mayor himself, which gives me authority to marry whoever I choose, and Miss Hall…" he paused, smiled and sighed deeply, "well, she sends me."

"Don't listen to him!" Kate fell to her knees pleading, "you mustn't believe him, my darling! Sylvain is a very suspicious character! He has just returned from The West Indies where it is rumored he learned to practice the voodoo necromancy of the islanders!"

"Why that's simply absurd," said Sylvain with a chuckle, "my friend Mr. Rigatoni here was by my side during the entire trip and not once did he see my practicing any Voodoo. Isn't that right, Mr. Rigatoni?"

He nudged the Italian with his elbow. The Italian slowly nodded his head. It looked like it required a lot of effort.

"Well, I'm satisfied." I wasn't. Nothing at this party was particularly satisfying. It was unsatisfying to the point at which the presence of Johnny Hideous and Skinny Valentine, who were attracted by the hubbub and now approaching me could almost be an entertaining diversion. Almost.

"This man givin' you trouble, Sylvain?" asked Johnny Hideous, his giant brow wrinkled with anger.

"We could make some serious trouble for him," Skinny chimed in, filing his nails with a switchblade.

I put my hand on my gun, expecting Sylvain to order them to rip me to shreds. He surprised me.

"Boy, you fellas sure are helpful but I think Jean could use some help down in the basement."

I couldn't help but snicker a little.

"Well, you heard the man. Jean could use some help down in the basement. I don't even know what you boys are doin' here anyway. Is Halperin too much of a coward to even come to parties?"

"Nah," Skinny spat at me, "he's just too important."

"Really?" I shot back, wishing I could do so literally, "if I'd known this was a party for people of no consequence I wouldn't have attended."

Hideous began to grind his teeth.

"Come on, Sylvain, you say the word and we'll pull out all this bear's stuffing…"

"Well, that's real generous Mr. Hideous, but I just don't think there's any call for acting like that. Mister Plush is a guest of the mayor and Jean is awful busy down there in the basement."

The second time he said it, it hit me.

"Jean's in the basement? Maybe I should…"

"No need, Mister Plush. You just enjoy the party. Johnny and Skinny can handle this, can't you, boys?"

"Yeah," said Skinny, awfully proud of himself, "we can handle it. You just enjoy the party."

Hideous gave me what he must have thought was a smile.

"You enjoy the party, Plush."

"Well now that you two mooks are out of the way, that should be a lot easier."

It was a weak quip. I wasn't feeling strong or confident or at all in control of the situation. I slinked away from Sylvain and Kate to rejoin the party, deciding that my famous magic act would turn the crowd in my favor.

As I was pulling a quarter out of old Mrs. Slocombe's ear, Chang was whispering into mine.

"I don't know if the people here are all alive."

I turned around to address him.

"Well, Chang that's to be expected at these society parties. You're just used to more interesting company than these rich stiffs. Chang, you've got to make an effort to integrate yourself more, like me with my magic."

"But, Mister Plush…"

"Chang, I am getting very tired of your cowardly and superstitious ways. You're an American now, Chang—well, not a real American, but you live in America and in America we're not very tolerant about cowardice and superstition. Immigrants need to keep their strange primitive beliefs back in the old country or else never become true Americans and be the subject of ridicule and the target of random but justified beatings. I will not have a coward who holds back the progress of the American Dream for a chauffeur."

My speech must have really affected him. His skin changed from yellow to white.

"M…m…mister Plush…."

"You know that I hate groveling Chang. I will have none of it."

"But m…m…m…m…" he was shaking.

I heaved a sigh.

"All right, Chang, maybe it was a little much for me to fire you. Now, calm down!"

Behind me, a horn honked several times.

"Hang on, pal, I'm lecturing my chauffeur!"

The horn honked again three times.

"I said, hang on, pal. Acts like he owns the road."

Somehow I felt as if something might actually be wrong.

"What's the matter, Chang?

Chang pointed over my shoulder.

"You know, Chang, it's not polite to point. Should I assume then, if you're pointing, something is very very wrong?"

He nodded.

"If I turn around, am I going to see something that's unspeakably terrifying?"

Honk honk. A nod from Chang. Against my better judgment, I turned around. I immediately stepped aside so the honker could get through. It was the curly haired rapist, still carrying his little horn. He had traded in his shabby trench coat for a new tuxedo which didn't do much to take your attention away from his mangled, caved-in face. If anything, by contrast it emphasized that he had been bashed to death against a wall. Dead men could walk *and* honk here.

41

"We've gotta get down to that basement." I couldn't keep my eyes off the curly haired dead man. I saw now what Sylvain was capable of and it certainly didn't bode well for either Jean or Kate. From Chang's body language he saw that my plan didn't bode well for him.

"Most honored Mister Plush, may I suggest instead we find the front door?"

The frightened chauffeur seemed about ready to take off in that very direction.

"Move another inch and you're actually fired. Also, I'll kill you." He didn't need to see the gun pointed at the back of his head. He knew me.

"This is a very bad idea. Very bad. This mansion is a dangerous place and there's only the two of us."

"Make it three," said Mittens, running to my side.

"I'll need you to get Sylvain away from his zombie slaves."

"I think I know just how to do it," said Mittens, "he seems to think he's a pretty big wheel, right?"

"He is a pretty big wheel," Chang replied, "even the dead respect him."

"Well, there isn't a man alive who thinks he's too important to talk to the press..." Mittens began to explain.

"With one exception of course," Chang interrupted.

"Of course," said Mittens, rolling his eyes, "nobody talks to him. He's the evilest man in town."

Chang nodded in agreement.

"Much more evil than Sylvain."

"Yes, much more." I wanted to move this along so pretended I knew who it was they were talking about. I'd have to ask Chang sometime.

"At any rate," said the frustrated kitty, "I'll give him an interview."

I patted his head. I didn't know if it was polite, patronizing or a homosexual advance, but I felt as if he deserved it.

"You're a good kitty, Mittens."

We fell silent like nothing existed but us three and the gravity of the situation. And this was a grave situation. The gravest I'd been in since I woke up as Jimmy Plush. Mittens stared at me in that way that only a cat could. It stung. He broke the silence.

"I'm in whatever this is until the end, but you're going to be sorry if you mess this up. You're the worst person I know and two women love you in spite of it. Do you know what happens to a man like you when he loses two women that love him, maybe that he actually loves?"

I could only shake my head "no". No it can't happen. No, I don't want to think about it. No, I can't imagine it. No, I don't know and I hope I never do.

"Neither do I, Plush." He walked off to find Sylvain. Chang and I blended in with the crowd as best we could, but kept our eyes and ears on him so we'd know when to follow him and make our move. A loud cat reporter in a tuxedo can get attention like few things in existence.

"Hey, Sylvain!" he shouted about two feet closer to the guy than would warrant shouting. Sylvain responded with a laugh and a big, dumb grin. Some voodoo priest he was.

"Well, hey yourself, little kitty. Is there somethin' I can do for ya? You want some milk?"

"Yes, Mister Sylvain, there most certainly is. I'm Mittens O' Hara from the Nero City Plain Dealer Gazette and I'm hoping to get an interview with you."

Sylvain's eyes and mouth grew.

"Shucks, me? Well that sounds just fine!'

"Excellent. Let's go someplace private," Mittens leaned in a bit closer, "I'm afraid your friend can't come with us."

Sylvain made an unpleasant face.

"Mister Rigatoni goes everywhere I go," Sylvain insisted, "with no exceptions."

"I'm afraid it's against Writer's Guild regulations to have an outsider present while doing an interview. I could lose my reporting license."

Sylvain hanged his head.

"Well, gee, I'd hate to get you in trouble, kittycat."

"So you'll do it?"

Sylvain rubbed Mittens' chin.

"Of course I will. Mr. Rigatoni, stay."

The Italian did just that, to startling effect. He could have easily been mistaken for a wax museum exhibit on organ grinders. Mittens and Sylvain headed for the coatroom and because the Italian had been told to stay, we walked past him without him so much as batting an eyelash.

As soon as all three of us were in the coatroom with Sylvain, we jumped him. He might have learned voodoo in the West Indies, but he didn't learn fighting anywhere. He literally fought like a girl with limpwristed slaps and clumsy, flailing kicks. He hit the floor fast and was undressed and searched for weapons just as quickly. Not so much as a pocketknife. We tied his hands together with his sock garters and took turns headbutting him in the face. After one round of this, he was gettin' awfully dizzy, very close to blacking out.

"Alright," he moaned, "I'll talk. What do you wanna know?"

"You can start with why you're doing this." I punched him in the gut to make sure he knew just how serious I was.

"I'm not doing this," he answered, "I don't know the first thing about voodoo. Up until a few days ago, I didn't know how to spell it. There's no voodoo goin' on here. It's somethin' different. I'm Larry Schultz. I'm an actor you've never heard of."

His story half checked out. I'd never heard of him. I still didn't understand.

"Would you mind clarifying that?'

"I've always wanted to be an actor ever since I saw Zeppo Marx in a movie. I always thought he was the funny one…"

I punched him in the gut again for that.

He had to take a little while to catch his breath.

"I wanted to be an actor but I could never get any good parts. I felt like a real loser, like I oughta put an end to my life. I realized that that pain was a lot like the pain Hamlet felt, you know, To Be or Not to Be and all that jazz. So I auditioned to play Hamlet. I wasn't so great. So, I went to the roof of the theater to jump off and kill myself. The director talked me down by sayin' he had a part for me. In Hamlet! I was hopin' for Horatio or Claudius but instead he cast me as the Frigidaire. I didn't even know there was a Frigidaire in Hamlet."

"There was one in Othello," said Mittens.

"That was a washing machine," I corrected him.

"My mistake."

"Everybody knows Hamlet's the one with the Frigidaire," Chang chided him.

I punched Larry Schultz in the gut again for his ignorance regarding the works of The Bard.

"Oof…please stop…let me finish, please. So, I'm playing a Frigidaire in Hamlet and there in the front row I see Miss Hall. And like I said, she sends me. But, what am I gonna do? I'm just a failed actor playing an appliance in a pretty poor production of Hamlet. Seeing happiness right in front of my eyes and knowing that it will never be mine is awful lot to take, so I climb to the theater roof again."

"Really? You seemed so cheery."

He smiled.

"Well, yeah, cause my life turned around. I was up there on the roof, thinkin' about how I had no prospects when a strange foreign man yells up at me. He says not to jump. He says he loved me in Hamlet and he says he's got a job for me. The role of a lifetime. I get to play the villain and still get the girl. Not an actor alive could turn down a choice part like that. Before you know it, the mayor's a zuvembie slave that signs anything, I got a marriage certificate and life is just fine. Bein' Sylvain beats bein' Larry Schultz any day!"

The end of his story actually proves helpful. I can finally put two and two together.

"Foreign, eh? Did he sound like he was Chinese? Chinese, but not Chinese?"

A perfect plan. I don't know how he managed to make the zombies but that doesn't matter. Everything else comes together. Getting rid of a whore that might prove to be a breach of security one day, making two henchmen that already have no brains into mindless slaves, controlling the mayor, taking the last little piece of the city he didn't have. Clever for once, Vic, clever. But you didn't count on your actor singin' like a canary.

"Nah," he answered, deflating my solution to the case, "he wasn't a Chinaman. He was from someplace else. I think it was…"

Before he could finish his thought, somebody was banging on the coatroom door.

"Just hang it on a chair!" I shouted at the rude son-of-a-bitch outside. Whoever it was must have been a real stickler for etiquette, since shortly after I said that, the door came crashing down revealing that Mr. Rigatoni and the curly-haired now faceless rapist were doin' the knocking and knocking down alike. They weren't alone. Standing right behind the two was a curvaceous mystery woman proudly sporting a crisp new tuxedo over her foxsuit and carrying Kate Hall over her shoulder.

"Help!" Kate screamed, "Mister Plush, save me!"

The zuvembie Jean didn't give me time to react. She only wanted to stand in the doorway and show me that they had Kate Hall and would probably kill her. Moving far faster than her brain-dead brethren, Jean and Kate were gone as fast as they came, leaving Rigatoni and the faceless rapist to deal with us. I had a sinking feeling that they might not have much trouble with it either. A feeling confirmed when the blonde came charging at me. Even though he was honking that goddamn horn of his, I still didn't have time to get out of the way and ended up feeling something pretty similar to the sensation the poor bicycle messenger must have felt earlier in the night, particularly as he ripped open my new stitches and began yanking stuffing out of my stomach.

Meanwhile, Chang was attempting to bring down Rigatoni before he could grab Sylvain. He came at the Italian with the Gilded Battleaxe Fist, a martial arts move known to make the strongest men drown in their own vital fluids. Hadn't seen anyone too tough to drown before, but there's a first time for everything. Chang hit two things during the early moments of the scrap—Rigatoni and the floor. Mittens surveyed the fight and did the logical thing, though probably for the wrong reason. Chang was full of blood which is hard to replace. I was full of stuffing and there were several sacks of it in the trunk. When it comes between seeing a man die and a toy break, it's obvious what people will choose. His hatred of me still had no small part in his choice. He dove onto Rigatoni's back, driving his claws as deep as he could. Rigatoni kept right on choking the Chinaman, which was not particularly shocking since he'd just taken a Gilded Battleaxe fist like it was nothing.

Sylvain wouldn't have been much good in the fight, even if he wasn't tied up. He was busy crying and soiling himself, filling a room that reeked of the stench of failure with the stench of human waste as well. I had been hoping perhaps he would be sensible enough to try and untie himself and dash out the door so he could provide me with some details on the goddamn mastermind behind this mess, which would not have been too much to expect of someone. He was only tied up with sock garters and that was almost entirely for dramatic effect. Sylvain instead twitched and cried and agitated the situation by vomiting at the stench of his shit. The faceless rapist let go of me, ran and honked his way over to Sylvain, threw the shit-stained naked actor over his shoulder and ran out the door. I was too busy recovering the stuffing I'd lost and shoving it back into me to do anything about it. On the plus side, Rigatoni shook Mittens off his back, let go of Chang and joined his friend on his trip to the basement. Not our finest moment.

"Come on! We've got to follow them!" It wasn't in our best interest but it was in Kate's. Jean was gone and I couldn't let her turn into one of those creatures too.

Chang laughed nervously.

"That's not such a good idea, Mister Plush. Following them might lead to catching up with them and we all know what happens then. Chang is loyal to the end but Chang is not stupid. I stay here."

Mittens gestured with a clawed paw.

"You're either a man or a mouse and you know what I do to mice."

"The Chinese do not fear cats," said Chang, folding his arms obstinately and holding his chin up in the air.

If I was to get him to come with me, I would have to use my superior mind.

"Come on, Mittens, let's go and leave him alone up here to wait for them to come back for him."

"Sounds like a plan, Plush," said Mittens with a wink, "let's leave the scaredy-cat alone."

"We'll deal with the zuvembies, Chang, you wait around here to deal with the ghosts."

Head hanging in resignation, the reluctant and frightened chauffeur joined our pursuit of Rigatoni and the faceless rapist. We trailed the two to a large library where they weaved through a maze of bookshelves until they came upon a statue of Spaulding, the famous mustachioed explorer of the Dark Continent. A fatter, balder man with a less impressive moustache stood beside it waiting. The man waved hello to Rigatoni and the faceless rapist. They did not wave hello back. He pulled down on the statue's mustache and a cage came down from the ceiling. Inside the cage was an emaciated old geezer, naked as a jaybird. He reached down his throat, gagged and vomited up a key, which he gave Rigatoni.

"Now bring it back when you're done with it," the old geezer said, wagging a bony finger.

The two wandered the surprisingly vast hallways of the mansion until they came to a door marked with a grinning skull. They put the key in the keyhole and opened it. The door led to a long, dark spiral staircase. I rushed down, accompanied by Mittens and Chang, not knowing how I would get Kate away from the zuvembies when I got there and not caring that I didn't know.

In the basement, a number of stiff socialites were gathered around four dead clowns lying on their stomachs. Strapped to the dead clowns were Kate, Sylvain, Johnny and Skinny. They were all wearing gas masks and all hooked up to a big machine shaped like a laughing devil's face, which was in turn hooked up to a big glass canister full of swirling mist, which was in turn hooked up to a console of some kind. Standing at the console, working its various levers was Professor Blasko, a mad scientist I had crossed swords with during my first case as Jimmy Plush. He looked pale and greenish but was otherwise the same crotchety-looking, hook-nosed darkeyed widows-peaked European I'd met before.

"Ah, Mister Plush, you have come to witness my final triumph!" Blasko laughed and pulled a switch, which jolted Johnny and Skinny with electricity.

"Help us, Plush!" Hideous wailed as the current sizzled his body.

"Yeah, help us!" Skinny echoed. He didn't look like he was holding up very well.

"The time has come to admit defeat," Blasko declared with a flourish, "the woman you love is one of my zuvembie slaves and your fiancée will soon join her!"

I observed the situation, took all of the factors into consideration and decided that the only course of action was to pull my gun. It was usually part of the solution to most of my problems. There were at least fifteen of them and we'd had trouble with two. A gun couldn't hurt, especially if it could hurt the zuvembies.

"Shooting me won't stop my plan, Mister Plush!" Blasko gloated, "My zuvembie slaves have been taught to make Kate Hall into one of them if anything happens to me. When she is one of my slaves, I will order her and the whore you once loved to tear you to pieces and rip the stuffing from you!"

It was time to seek less orthodox solutions.

"And what if I shot that suspicious looking glass canister?"

"Then you would be a fool!" Blasko shouted. Blasko did a lot of shouting. "The Hall family once ran this mansion as a hospital for bearded babies and their unquiet, bearded souls have haunted the Halls for generations! The machine agitates their etheric energy, using it as a power source for my Relivineating gas, which I have used to create my zuvembie slaves. Breaking open that tank of ghosts would be foolish even for you."

"I think you're bluffing," I said nonchalantly and shot the tank. He wasn't. Who could have seen that coming? Men in that position are usually bluffing. The bullet made a little crack but little cracks in things like a glass canister or a relationship or a man's heart grow big fast. And when a big crack grows, it reaches everything and when everything's cracked and there's no time to fix it, it ain't long before everything's broken. And when a heart or a relationship or a glass canister get broken, things spill out into the world.

There were about a dozen babies—little, round and terrible things. They had beards—big, black, furry Cossack affairs, thick and crawling with maggots. Their eyes had rotted from their sockets but behind there was a glow—a glow of terrible wrongness and blinding hate. They first flew to the zuvembies, who they looked at as a travesty of death. They grabbed their heads, turning them with a strength you really wouldn't expect from babies and screwing them off as if they hadn't been put on tight enough. When the heads were detached, still bearing the same blank, stupid expression the babies squeezed them and they popped, making a disgusting mess worse than that made by Hideous when he tossed the faceless rapist against the wall. They squealed and cooed and clapped with pleasure at the destruction they'd caused.

When they got to Jean, it was too much. I knew what was underneath the foxhead wasn't Jean, but it hurt anyway. It hurt not just because I was seeing a woman I'd once loved turned into a bloody gooey mess by bearded phantom babies but because I was reminded that this was one of the few times I could tell what was inside of her head and what had been inside of that suit. I didn't have any time to grieve. From what Blasko had said about the ghosts, I knew who they'd be after next and I couldn't let them get her.

I ran like God, the Devil and the IRS were at my back, then made a flying leap that took full advantage of my lack of mass. I covered most of the distance I needed. Most of it. By the time, I made it to the clowns the ghosts had done it. For ages, they'd longed for the blood of the Hall family and they got it. I was just in time to get splattered with bone fragments and blood from my fiancée's head . My brain slipped away from me, my perceptions clouded over. I did something only someone confused, numbed by grief and desperate for some kind of familiarity would do—I saved the lives of two bastards I hated.

Hideous scowled at me as I untied him. It was as much gratitude as I expected.

"This don't change anything! Next time we meet, you're dead, Jimmy Plush, you're dead!'"

"Good!" I said, now full of hate and anger where the confusion and numbness had been, "with enemies like you as friends, who needs enemies? Scram! I've got business here."

Chang finished untying Skinny and pleaded with me with his slanty eyes.

"We must go, now, Mister Plush. The spirits are close and remaining here will only bring you closer to death."

The spirits were unscrewing Sylvain's head. They'd go for Blasko next.

"I can't go. Chang, Mittens, Johnny, Skinny, run for it."

Mittens hesitated.

"I don't know if I can let you stay here."

"Scat, cat! The rest of you too!"

And they did. There was just me, Blasko and the ghosts now. Blasko was cowering behind his machine and the bearded ghost babies were going to unscrew his head. I couldn't allow that to happen.

"Stop!" I yelled at the ghosts and they stopped. Neither of us expected it.

"This man might have wronged you, but he's wronged me worse. This man is responsible for the deaths of not one but two women that I loved. And I think he might have invented whatever it was that made me a teddy bear and my...friend a cat. And if he did that, he helped turn a good cop into a horse too. Between what this man did and what he might have done, he's got suffering to do. This man is mine!"

The ghosts spoke with a single voice like the quintuplets outside the carnival, except that they sounded like baritone babies.

"As you wish. We shall move on to our eternal resting place." They made a "poof" noise and were gone.

As they vanished from sight, I felt something difficult to describe, other than that it was disgusting. I had either intimidated or reasoned with creatures like that. Could it have been that they saw something of themselves in me? It was a scary thought. It's scary to think you're something scary. It's scarier that underneath the disgust you feel you've got every right to be scary. More so than I did the day before. I would have felt sorry for Blasko, having to face me when I'm in this state. I would have if I hadn't used up the last of my pity on Johnny and Skinny.

"Get up!" I roared.

He got up. People don't expect a teddy bear to roar.

This basement had to be nothing but a temporary laboratory and he must have had something bigger and more glamorous elsewhere.

"Give Chang directions to your lab and no tricks."

"Yes," he moaned, drained by the whole ordeal, "no tricks."

He gave Chang directions to a warehouse on the docks, which to my surprise was not full of Zuvembie thugs ready to dismember me. It was actually just full of junk; devices that did nothing but generate bouncing arcs of lightning or flashing lights, severed robot heads that did nothing but repeat the time and weather and poorly gaffed dead sideshow freaks like a duck with antlers and five squirrels sewn together. The only thing of note were some giant canisters identical to the ones in the mayor's basement.

I tapped one of the giant canisters.

"So, is this the gas?"

"Yes, that's the gas, but it's only a prototype. It's worthless really. The subjects all showed sensitivity to pain. They were of no use to me."

I faked a yawn.

"Fascinating, I've got more questions."

"Yes, Plush, I'll answer anything you want."

"I know you know I'm not the real Jimmy Plush."

Blasko cackled like a maniac. I had to slap him to get him to stop.

"Yes, Hatbox, I know who you are. And yes, I did this to you."

I breathed in and out, in and out. Begged myself to talk instead of shoot so I wouldn't lose the opportunity to be myself again.

"Then if I brought you the real Jimmy Plush, could you switch us back?"

I was in a bad position. If the answer to the question was yes, I'd have to gamble on him telling the truth, which had to be one-in-a-million. A man in this position who valued his skin would give a "yes", true or otherwise.

"The body switch process is irreversible."

I didn't like hearing that. Saved me some disappointment, though, and surprised me a good deal.

"You're the most honest criminal I've ever met, Blasko."

"A scientist is a seeker of the truth not a perpetrator of lies!"

"Why'd you go this far?" It's odd how much morbid

curiosity I possessed. Why is it there's nothing more interesting than knowing exactly why your life's been ruined again? In my mind, I'd pulled the trigger about four times already.

"I wanted to pay you back for killing me before. Nobody kills Arizstid Blasko!"

"I think that statement's about to become a lie twice over, Blasko."

He folded his hands like he was standing before his maker. It was a little early for that, if a man like him would ever get the privilege, that is.

"Wait!" he said, his eyes tearing up, "I didn't come up with this plan! I'm innocent! I was given a briefcase of money by a man in a police uniform. Officer Berry, John Berry. The same officer brought me the whore for this party. I don't know who sent him, I swear! Please, spare my life, Plush! I repent for my sins! I repent! Let me live!"

I chuckled ominously.

"Don't worry, you'll live."

I pistol-whipped Blasko unconscious then strapped him to his machine. Reading this man's notes wasn't easy. I had to phone around town to find somebody that read funny Russian squiggles and spoke Hungarian that had no problem coming out to a mysterious warehouse laboratory at four in the morning. Blasko woke up and got knocked out four times before I managed that small miracle. Then I had to call a scientist out to calibrate the machine according to the instructions. Then I had to shoot the tutor and tell the scientist at gunpoint to keep his mouth shut. Then I had to wait for Blasko to wake up so that he could feel the life energy draining out of him and the Relivineating gas overtaking him. Then, I had to shoot the scientist. Maybe I didn't have to, but I felt like it and most of the time, I try to do what I feel like because that's what people expect of Jimmy Plush. God knows what people would expect of a bereaved, angry Jimmy Plush. In my head, Mittens kept saying that I was the worst man he knew.

After the fifth or sixth time killing Blasko, I stopped caring. His screaming was almost unbearably loud while I spent three days skinning him and sticking safety pins into his exposed organs.

I left him in his lab, strapped down and squirming in pain forever and walked off to find the man who had to be behind the corrupt cops that brought Jean to Blasko, the man who financed his damned experiments. The cops in this town bowed down to Vic Halperin. The time had come to finally put an end to The Pale Peril.

Mr. Plush and
the Chief Inspector

I was feeling tired, angry, sad. Dead inside. I was feeling like I was stuffed with lead and roaches instead of cotton. Chang had offered to sew up my stitches, but I didn't feel whole, so there was no reason to look that way, no reason to act like it would heal. Nothing was going to heal me but Vic Halperin's heart in my hand so I could squeeze the blood out like he'd done to me.

"Chang is worried, most honored Mister Plush. Chang does not believe that Halperin was behind the incident."

I slapped him, then I pistol-whipped him in the face.

"Chang does not tell most honored Mister Plush how to be a detective. This trench coat, this hat, this phony goddamn job are all most honored Mister Plush has! And most honored Mister Plush is going to take it out of the man that took it from him. Who did Hatbox owe so much money to? Halperin. Who made my girlfriend a whore? Halperin! Who makes this town too damn dismal to live in? Victor Halperin, that's who!"

It's a sad state of affairs when a man is almost too tired for a massacre.

"You're going to lose all your stuffing." That was all he said. Made me mad. Made me want to hit him again. But damned if he wasn't the only one looking out for me now.

"Get the bag from the car."

"And the sewing kit?"

"No time for that."

"Everyone has time to stay alive."

I shook my head.

"Halperin and his mooks don't. So get me the damn bag from the car."

Chang got the damn bag. I grabbed a wad of stuffing and shoved it in. I don't think it was in there particularly tight, but I couldn't care less about all that. There was nothing I wouldn't mind losing except for a chance at revenge.

I kicked open the door and shot the maître d' in the gut.

"Is there something…" He was holding his gunshot wound, but didn't cease to be a perfect maître d'.

"Yeah, there's something you can do for me. Take your hand off the wound. I gutshot you because I wanted to see ya bleed. Don't disappoint a little bear with a gun who wants nothing more than to kill you. You might live if you crawl bleeding to your boss. If you don't crawl and you ain't bleeding, you won't live."

The maître d' got down on his wounded belly and started to crawl to the back of the restaurant. Nobody stood up. Everyone here knew where they were eating and knew that it was just a matter of time before something like this happened. Some of them were also smart enough to know that when I start shooting, I don't like to stop. It's one of my less pleasant features. Today, I really didn't feel like putting my best foot forward.

Halperin himself didn't come out with the crawling Maître d'. Instead, his right and left hand men, Johnny Hideous and Skinny Valentine did.

"You got a problem, Plush?" Hideous asked with an impressive sneer.

"You remember the soiree?"

"Yeah, what about it?" Skinny tried to look tough.

"That night I saved your lives. And I ain't Chinese. I believe when you save a man's life, it's yours to take back whenever the hell you please. Do you know what that means?"

Skinny appeared shaken.

"I ain't afraid of you, little bear."

"Well, you should be. And you should be scared of a man that left you two to be turned into mindless undead slaves."

Skinny and Johnny both put hands on their chins, visibly pondering my words.

"So, boys, are you more obligated to a man that left you for dead or one that's saved your life and will kill you if you try to protect the man that left you for dead."

They shook, but continued to appear obstinate.

"Pair of cupcakes like you might not know what it's like to lose a woman, but I've lost two. If either of you got enough humanity in you to let a grieving man deal with his pain, I suggest you back away from that door. Otherwise, my pain becomes yours and I've got a lot of pain in me right now."

I was being real fair to those two and they finally knew it, in fact they marched into Halperin's office side by side with me. Not only side by side, but Hideous went in first.

Hideous approached Halperin's oversized desk and pounded it with his oversized fist.

"You sold us out, Vic! You sold us all out!"

I drew my gun and took aim at Halperin's head while he was distracted. With Blasko I felt like torturing him and making him feel everything I'd felt. Halperin on the other hand, I just wanted dead.

If I'd blinked, I'd have missed the events that occurred a second later. I fired my gun. Hideous grabbed for Halperin's throat. Halperin grabbed Hideous' arm with one hand and tossed him over his shoulder into the giant gong behind his desk He reached out with his other hand and grabbed my bullet before it hit him. The gong made a "bonnngggg" noise because somebody had just smacked into it. Skinny Valentine fled screaming. It was a very eventful second.

I was kind of scared of the guy after that. I still felt like killing him but he'd just displayed a level of skill in the Chinese fighting arts that an actual Chinaman would be jealous of. I squeezed off three more shots, which he swatted from the air like insects. And suddenly, he was standing in front of me, looking me in the face.

"Most honored, Plush," he said, "I am aware why you have come here. And were I the man responsible for your loss—and I am not—you would be most justified in shooting me down. But, of course, I don't need to tell you that and I think we've known each other long enough to know that you don't give a damn about justice, but rather are ruled by a series of petty, violent impulses that would be embarrassing for a small child, let alone a distinguished private investigator."

For some reason, I was listening to him. I was trembling, scared of an enemy I'd always thought of as quite pathetic. What kind of man pretends to be Chinese all day?

"I'm still going to kill you." I had to say it. Whether I'd do it or not was up for debate. Whether I could or not, even.

57

"That's all well and good, but we have a mutual antagonist it seems."

"I always knew from your damn gaudy décor that you secretly hated yourself, Vic."

Halperin put a finger against his temple massaging it.

"Someone is causing me great stress. Someone is hurting my operation, giving my girls over to the police. You know what happens when the police get a hold of people in this city. I didn't send Jean to the soiree. She was taken off the street and brought there. I did not sell out my men. I am not a traitor and I am not as crooked as you think I am. I want you to find this man."

I holstered my gun.

"If there is such a man, I want me to find him too."

"Good. Then go to Muffinhead Howard's on the docks. Find Bulgy O' Toole and the Ritz Brothers. Put some fear into them. They know you. They know you, they'll talk."

So, that was it, I turned around and left the office, but not before addressing Halperin one more time.

"I just want you to remember this: I don't work for you, you son-of-a-bitch."

Chang was waiting for me in the car.

"Did you kill him?"

"He didn't do it. We need to go to Muffinhead Howard's by the docks. You know the place?"

"Yes and so do you."

"Tell me then. And tell me how I know Bulgy O' Toole and The Ritz Brothers."

"Some time ago, a very bad man needed a shipment protected from Halperin. He was, in fact, not just a bad man, he was the worst man in town."

I couldn't begin to conceive of the worst man in this town.

"Do you think he has something to do with this case?"

Chang stifled a laugh.

"The tiger need not whisper. When an elephant takes a step, everybody hears it."

How very Chinese of him.

"So what was this shipment?"

"A Sexquatch."

"Oh, just a Sexquatch? Why all the commotion then?"

Yes, that was sarcasm. I don't know how he expected me to know what a Sexquatch was.

"A Sexquatch is exactly what it sounds like, a lady sasquatch trained in the arts of pleasure. Halperin wanted it for himself, so Plush was hired to protect it. Bulgy O'Toole and The Ritz Brothers were hired to steal it. They were not successful. Worse still, Plush took the Sexquatch for himself, used it until he got tired of it then, posing as a meat salesman named Isaac Bickerstaff Jenkins sold the Sexquatch's meat to Halperin for use at J.L Wong's. Halperin thought it was perfectly edible cat meat. But Sexquatch meat causes hallucinations and vomiting and there was a food critic in the restaurant when it went out. Halperin fired Bulgy and killed one of the Ritz Brothers for failing him."

I shuddered thinking about the person everybody believed I was.

"And Muffinhead Howard?"

"Mister Plush briefly dated Muffinhead Howard's sister."

"Assuming that Muffinhead Howard is called Muffinhead Howard because he has a muffin for a head, that's pretty disgusting."

"No. His sister had a snickerdoodle for a head."

That made a bit more sense. Snickerdoodles are a very sensual cookie.

"That one I can understand. She sounds cute."

"She was, until he got tired of her and bit her head off."

That was disgusting.

"How could you work for a man like that?"

Chang shrugged.

"Hard to find good jobs for Chinese in this town. They fired me from kitchen of J.L Wong's."

That was more disgusting.

So, there I was at Muffinhead Howard's. I was a bear hell-bent on finding his girl and this was where my shifty pseudochinese archnemesis had sent me. It was about what I expected, blackjack games, crap games, poor lighting, a guy in a cougar suit taking wagers on a wrestling match between two dwarves and a monitor lizard. As I was putting twenty on the lizard, the man behind the bar caught sight of me. It should have been hard to tell, him being the aptly named proprietor of Muffinhead Howard's and therefore having a muffin for a head (unless two of those blueberries happened to be his eyes) but the way he stroked his shotgun like it was his manhood and Veronica Lake had just walked in to dry off her angora sweater was kind of a giveaway. I'd have to tread lightly here...who the hell am I kidding? No, I wouldn't.

I scanned the room for Bulgy O' Toole and the Ritz Brothers. Siamese twins, one dead, one a vaudevillian with a penchant for lime green suits and a guy with eyes the size of baseballs didn't take me long to pinpoint. It didn't take Bulgy long to pinpoint me either. With those eyes, why would it?

"Don't you know you're unwelcome here?" he tried to splash his drink on me, but was a poor judge of distance and missed me by a couple inches.

"Come on, if I only went where I was welcome, I'd be cooped up in my office all week and what fun would that be?"

"That would suit us just fine," said Spanky Ritz, the putrescent half of the team. He didn't stink half as bad as his brother's ventriloquism.

I jumped on their table, took aim and shot Muffinhead Howard before he could cock his shotgun. I didn't like the idea of my guts inside of four different pillows, thank you very much. There were crumbs and blueberry ink everywhere and the blackjack game stopped for a whole ten seconds.

Bulgy laughed nervously.

"You think that scares me, Plush?"

"It scares me," said Spanky Ritz.

His brother slapped him.

"Shut up, this is serious!"

Spanky blew a surprisingly convincing raspberry at his living sibling.

"You know, dad never loved you!"

"You shut up!"

Growing tired of sibling rivalry, I reunited the act with my custom teddy bear .45, which I then fired at the ceiling to get the bar's attention.

Bulgy vomited on himself. Then sat up and tried to act tough again.

"I'm not scared, Plush! I'm not telling you nothing!"

I ignored him.

"Anybody here eating spaghetti?" I yelled.

A nervous little man brought me a plate, heaping with sauce and meatballs. Bulgy laughed. Nervously. The only way a guy being interrogated like this could laugh.

"Trying to bribe me with food? It won't work."

I picked up a fork off the table, jammed it into one of Bulgy's big fat eyeballs and yanked hard. It was not a pretty sight, but luckily for Bulgy he only caught it from the left. I took the fork with Bulgy's fat right eye on it and twirled it around in the spaghetti. I pointed my gun at Bulgy's face as I moved the fork toward his mouth.

"Eat up, have a nice juicy meatball."

Realizing he wasn't ever going to get the eye back in and a moment of degrading and nauseating himself again was better than being dead, he agreed and began enjoying the worst mouthful of spaghetti he'd ever eaten. I waited until he was finished before gestutring toward his left eye with the fork.

Unless you want seconds, you're gonna talk. I wanna know why the cops broke the deal with Halperin, I wanna know what's under that giant black cloth and I sure as hell wanna know where they took my girl. You'd better talk fast. That empty eye socket's really disgusting."

Bulgy threw up on himself once more.

"Is this the thanks I get? I serve you a perfectly good eyeball and you throw it right back up! Let's see if the other one tastes better."

"Townsquare Vanzetti," he blurted out.

"Could you be more specific? Are you tellin' me something or are you ordering more pasta?"

"He's under the big black tent. He's gigantic and he's come to help Vic Halperin reclaim some of his territory."

"So why would he be handing Furry hookers over to the police?"

Bulgy shrugged.

"Maybe they don't know who belongs to Halperin and who belongs to Kewpie Doll Steve."

"Would he have a reason to kill Horskowitz?"

"Maybe. A lot of people had reason to kill the horse. Halperin, Kewpie Doll Steve, the police themselves. He put me away for a year, if it wasn't for me tasting bad that would have been the end of me."

I didn't bother to say goodbye. I'm sure everyone was heartbroken, but I had to get to the "carnival", see if something more sinister than a little hanky-panky in the tunnel of love was going down. When I got there, the pinstriped quintuplets were standing guard as before.

"Good day, sir," they said in unison, "is there something we can do for you?"

"Yeah, there is. How much for a ticket?"

They whispered among themselves. Didn't look as if many people tried to get into this carnival.

"Six thousand dollars," they said, their tones very adamant.

"Seems like a lot of money for a carnival."

"Yes, it is. So leave."

"Must be a hell of a carnival, though."

"No, it's quite awful."

I drew my gun and shot the quint in the chest. Either I draw fast or he thought I was going for my checkbook. As he reeled in pain from the gunshot wound, his brothers charged me, halberds in hand.

"Hell of a town this is," I said, as I jumped, flipped and shot at them at the same time, "guy can't go to the carnival without fat miscreants attacking him with obscure medieval weaponry."

With the knowledge I had of the Chinese fighting arts and my impressive skill with my custom teddy bear .45, it was only a matter of seconds before I caught the injured one in the heart and another one of them in the leg. When this one hobbled his way into the path of a karate chop to the base of the spine, the three surviving quints decided they might just get cooperative.

"What do you want?"

"I want to talk to Vanzetti."

"There is no such person, this is a carnival."

I stood my ground.

"You know there is and you know I'm willing to kill to talk to him. Show me your boss."

"Well done, Mister Plush, the stories of your detective skills are not exaggerated."

One of the quints pulled a small radio out of his pocket.

"This is Number three at the carnival, Mister Vanzetti has business."

A small squadron of tiny airplanes brought down hooks to lift the black cloth, revealing a man big enough to be passed off as a small carnival. He was less of a man than a series of enormous folds and wrinkles underneath a white robe that it must have taken a village to sew. Beside him was a telescope pointed upward. I glanced through it and could see a confident, judgmental aristocratic face. He was wearing a red fez that might have been a danger to low flying aircraft. Next to the telescope was a telephone that connected to a series of cables coiled around a large scaffold. At the top of this scaffold was a horn shaped earpiece.

I picked up the telephone. What came out should have been something like "I know what you've done, you sonofabitch and I don't care how big you are, I will rip out your heart and feast on it!" What came out was less assertive.

"Hello? Mister Vanzetti?"

"Well look at this," said the giant mobster in a thunderclap voice, "Jimmy Plush, the world's only teddy bear detective. To what do I owe the honor?"

"You owe the honor to two dead mooks and three thugs smart enough to play my game. You'd do well to think like the latter."

"You're an impertinent little bear, Plush. I dislike impertinent little bears and I dislike threats. Threats against someone of my...." he chuckled to himself, so I knew what was coming next.

"...Stature are nothing but tiny little insects to be swatted away. I can swat you away so easily, Plush. I can swallow you whole, I can send you miles away just by breathing on you. Why should I do anything for you?"

He was right. He was the size of a mountain, I was the size

of a toddler. Why should he be afraid of me? It would take an elephant gun to shoot this guy, and by an elephant gun I mean a gun that fires elephants.

"Because I'm the size of a small child and I'm still willing to mouth off. So I must know something that you don't about my giant killing capabilities."

He laughed a truly patronizing laugh.

"You don't frighten me, Mr. Plush, but you certainly amuse me. I'll answer your questions, gumshoe."

"Okay, tell me why Halperin's girls keep getting caught by the cops."

He growled a little. Well, as much as a man his size could do anything a little.

"Cops? What do you think I know about cops? All I know is I like to squash 'em. That Chief Inspector bugs me. I don't deal with the cops in this town and Vic Halperin's a friend of mine. Townsquare Vanzetti is good to his friends and death to his enemies, he does not allow his associates to be taken to prison and eaten. Good day to you, Mister Plush, lest you yourself clog up my bowels with cheap fabric."

A lot of people have made a sucker out of me in my time but I can usually tell when somebody's lying to my face. This guy wasn't lying to my face. This guy would eat any cop that went near him and would expect any redblooded American to do the same thing. He was genuinely enraged at the idea he'd be in league with the local constabulary. As bold as I was, I wasn't going to accuse a giant crime boss of lying to me, especially when I was almost completely certain he wasn't. I didn't know who was behind Jean and Kate's murder anymore, which should have made me angry. It didn't. Common sense told me that it's in anyone's best interest for the object of their vendetta to not be several stories tall.

"Well, thank you for your time, Mr. Vanzetti. Don't eat anyone I wouldn't eat."

I returned to the limo to find Chang unconscious in the driver's seat. Before I could open the door and get a closer look, I felt a tiny sting in my back and I was starting to get real drowsy real fast. Both the fighting and the questioning had been pretty leisurely, so I deduced that it was some kind of narcotic that had me tuckered out so quickly. There was a dart sticking out of my back. Before I could get out, I was out cold.

When I awakened, I was tied to one of three tables. There was a policeman standing at one of the others picking the intestines out of a dead whore dressed as a praying mantis. The suit had been ripped open so he could get at the organs he needed, but he'd kept the head on her. It was probably for the best that there were no holes in the big red velour compound eyes for a person to see out of for real. The cop was dripping with blood and shit and there was a big smile on his ravenous piggy face. On the third table, a cop was on top of a second dead whore. This one's suit had once been a pig, but it had been torn open and the head removed. He was thrusting viciously into her as he ripped skin off her face with his teeth.

I had a feeling I would not relish what was going to happen to me next. This feeling was validated by the arrival of one of the quintuplets I had seen guarding the giant tarp.

"You should have stayed out of this. Now you've gone and antagonized the police. We endured your foolishness for so long without having to step in and now, we'll have no more of it. Don't panic, Mr. Plush, we're not going to kill you."

"Who's panickin'?" I couldn't quite muster the Jimmy Plush bravado as I said it.

"Officer Berry, get the plaid and the scissors."

The piggy faced cop who'd been eating the mantis-hooker reluctantly abandoned his cannibalistic activities.

"Hmmph, I've gotta do everything around here!"

He sashayed toward a file cabinet in a fat, stupid, effeminate, waddly fashion. He soiled himself and laughed at the stench of stinking human flesh diarrhea. This felt like another one of those situations in which a good faint would save me a lot of misery. So, I fainted.

When I woke up, I saw that first of all, my right arm was made of pink plaid. It was terrible to have a plaid right arm. All around bad news. Before I could come to terms with this bad news, I had to face other bad news. I was tied to a beef jerky stick to be fed to the Chief Inspector. The Chief Inspector was another man so enormous, he took up an entire side of the street. I would've suspected the Chief Inspector could be none other than Townsquare Vanzetti, but his stylish raincoat and wool trousers gave the illusion of an upright man instead of a shady robed and fezzed criminal. At least this time I'd be eaten by an American instead of some grubby foreigner. So would Chang who was also tied to a beef jerky stick and wouldn't have to wait long after I was devoured to be eaten. The Chief Inspector took me in his giant, smelly hand and raised me slowly up to his mouth.

As the hand lifted me up to the Chief Inspector, I noticed there was something funny about his fake moustache, something real funny. I might not be much of a detective, but I made the connection pretty quickly; see, a few weeks ago, somebody broke into the zoo and stole a Brazilian furred anaconda, a gigantic hairy snake that spends most of the year hibernating, a snake big enough to serve as a fake moustache for a man who takes up an entire side of the street. All Vanzetti had to do was lift the snake up to his lip and it would sleep on his face, serving as a fake moustache (with the help of some double-sided tape.) Thus, all I would have to do to prove to the coppers that the man they worked for and the man they were chasing was to reveal to them that Vanzetti's moustache was actually a giant snake. He stole my life, so I was going to steal one of his.

I let the hand bring me up to the giant's mouth, but instead of just letting myself get eaten, I made a well timed jump onto the moustache, which I began beating savagely. Brazilian furred anacondas might sleep deeply, but they don't sleep through a flurry of well timed and surgically executed attacks utilizing the Chinese fighting arts. The snake woke up and it was mad. It wriggled free of the double sided tape, dropped down onto the Chief Inspector's lip and attempted to buck me off its back. Should have worked since I was a three foot bear and it was a furred anaconda but one of the twelve pillars of the Chinese fighting arts is balance. I kept on its back as it slithered along the Chief Inspector's lip and pounded it ferociously.

It came to realize that it wasn't going to knock me off by bucking, so it decided to rear up its ugly furry, snakey head to swallow me whole. I took this opportunity to take a truly stupid risk, to try to get it to the fall to the ground, revealing it as a fake.

The snake struggled valiantly, but I struggled even more valiantly and had all the rage a teddy bear with a plaid right arm has at his disposal. Giant snake or no giant snake, the advantage was mine.

The coppers were astonished to see the Chief Inspector's moustache fall to the ground – hard, with me on top. There it lay, twitching and dying from the fall. This was not the sort of behavior people expected from a moustache. It was confusing, and when confused, cops usually charge at people with their nightstick. One of the policemen on the scene began to do so.

"Wait!" I shouted, holding up my arms.

"You killed the Chief Inspector's moustache. Why should I wait?"

"Because if you look at the Chief Inspector's face without the moustache, you'll find he's Townsquare Vanzetti."

The policeman put his hand on his chin and lit a pipe. He was the type of policeman that liked to smoke a pipe when he was thinking.

"Perhaps I should examine this through the telescope."

"That's a very bad idea," said the surviving quintuplets, "you don't want to do that."

The policeman took his hand off his chin and looked into the telescope, shaking his head in disbelief at what he saw.

"My god, this is horrifying!"

"What is it?" asked one of his cohorts. The surviving quintuplets were shaking in their boots.

"Why, it seems that the Chief Inspector was none other than our archenemy Townsquare Vanzetti!"

The other policeman, upon hearing this, fainted dead away, their fragile, unbalanced minds unable to take the truth. It wasn't just fear of the cops that kept people from going to them for help. The human flesh was starting to get to their brains. The policeman dashed to the car, pursued by the surviving quintuplets. Chang, who had just regained consciousness and untied himself plowed through the other two quintuplets like a Chinese lawnmower... well, maybe not like a Chinese lawnmower because when Chang did it, it worked, and a Chinese lawnmower probably doesn't work at all. Whatever the case, the quintuplets were down and the cop had reached his car.

The policeman returned moments later with a few more policemen and a small band of mobsters and lowlives. They took turns looking up through the telescope and were all hopping mad to find out that Vanzetti had turned out to also be the Chief Inspector. This kind of deception would not stand in the sensible, honest world of organized crime. They left and returned with more thugs and some shopkeepers angry that they were paying protection money to the police, which would not stand. All of this of course, led to total chaos and a large mob assembling.

It looked as if most of the town's citizenry had gathered with torches, pitchforks, rocks, guns, cars and trucks. A hook and ladder company, several catering vans and a small squadron of airplanes had assembled along with several hundred representatives to stand against the colossus of corruption that had played everybody for saps. I decided it was best not to watch the fruits of my labor but instead to get to a safe distance. Probably a good idea because a guy like Vanzetti hitting the ground and getting dragged into the ocean by half the town was a real ruckus, and at three feet tall, as much as I love a ruckus, there's a good chance I'll get squished, immolated or torn to shreds during it.

The next day when whatever was done to Vanzetti by the vengeful city was done to him and everybody could get their bearings again, there was a knock on my door. It was a cop, cap in hand, face contrite. I was in no mood to see any representatives of law and order from this town.

"Get off my property," I said, brandishing my gun in the tacky plaid right arm the cops had given me.

"I'm here to make you an offer, Mister Plush."

I yawned. I laughed. I yawned again. I fired my gun in the air.

"Are you offering to get the hell out of my sight?"

"Well, umm…no sir."

"Then chances are, I'm likely to decline your offer."

The cop laughed.

"Well, sir, I don't think you are. It's a doozy of an offer."

Hmm. Something better than leaving me alone? Was he going to hang himself when he was done leaving me alone? Were he and his colleagues going to jump into the ocean?

"Okay, then, what's goin' on?"

"With the Chief Inspector exposed as Townsquare Vanzetti and Horskowitz, the best candidate for the job dead now, we'd like for you to take on the job."

Me? Representing law and order in this city? A bit farfetched. I had often fought on the side of the angels, but both law and order had never been a part of my methods. Especially not now, after the law had taken Jean and Kate from me. Chief Inspector Plush didn't sound good at all. It wasn't going to happen.

"I'm going to respectfully decline."

The policeman hanged his head.

I put my hand on my chin.

"Actually…"

The cop perked up, waiting for me to finish my sentence.

"I'm just going to decline."

I shot the cop in the face three times. From all the grief the Nero City police department had given me, it felt good. Not good enough though. Only one thing would make me feel good enough. I let the new stitches set in then headed to the police station where I was going to show this city's police force that nobody gives Jimmy Plush a plaid right arm then offers him a cushy job he doesn't want.

When I got to the police station, it turned out somebody had gotten the idea before I had. Every cop in town was dead in a heap, riddled with bullets. The culprit was still at the scene of the crime, looking awfully pleased. He had only beaten me to the punch because it was the sort of thing Jimmy Plush would do, and he had been Jimmy Plush long before I had.

"Well, well," I said, reaching for my gun, "if it isn't Jimmy Plush."

He shook his head "no."

"You must be mistaken, Mister Plush. Clearly you've taken a few too many bullets in your fuzzy wuzzy little head. You, sir, are Mister Plush. My name is Hatbox. Does it ring any bells? Surely a great teddy bear detective like yourself can figure it out."

"Well, Plush, I've gotta hand it to you, you sure are a great archnemesis. Killing a man's enemies for him? That's the work of a real Professor Moriarty. You know what I'd really hate? If you paid my electric bill or set J.L Wong's on fire. Looks like I'm not the one with a head full of stuffing after all."

He wagged a finger at me.

"How can a man walking around in my body, whose body I walk around in now underestimate me so? I did this to remind you of something."

"That policemen aren't bulletproof? Thanks, but I figured that one out myself. That these men deserved to die for working for the man that for no good reason arranged for the woman I love to die? Knew that. You confuse me, Plush."

"No. I wanted to prove that I'm a better you no matter which you I am. I know every petty little move you want to make, every little bullet riddled tantrum, you furry little frustrated id. A tiny facsimile of a bear, a tiny facsimile of a man. Silly, tragic, stupid. You're no better than the hired gun. All you can do is shoot. No matter how much you shoot and how much you hate, you'll never be able to hate as well as I can. Even at the one thing you have left, you're a failure. You weren't good enough at loving to protect Jean and Kate from the police and you're not good enough at hate to stop me from undermining anything important to you, which I can do at my leisure. Like now, for example. Your grief was important to you but all you're going to think about now that we've met again is hurting me real bad. I'm going to take off on the next boat to London. And your love and your grief will fade away. And to really hammer my point home, I'm going to fill you with holes."

He might have been a bastard, but he was no liar. I was going to need a lot more stitches and I couldn't think about a damn thing but seeing him dead.

Author's Note:

During the pulp magazine era, it was greatly en vogue to burn large piles of fiction so future generations would be confused or disappointed. This made a lot of sense to us because young people were getting ruder and dumber and didn't seem to deserve the benefit of our genius. How could we have known back then that this cool, sexy practice could come back and bite us in the ass? Nowadays, it doesn't seem like such a valid excuse and because we didn't have Rap Music, MySpace and videogames to make us dumber, we look pretty ridiculous for it. There are a couple gaps in the narrative between Mr. Plush and the Chief Inspector and Jimmy Plush in the Tomb of the Martian Pharaoh, but I'm sure these will not impede your understanding or enjoyment too much as the plot of the eight stories between Chief Inspector and Tomb of the Martian Pharaoh flowed smoothly and did not really introduce a lot of new elements.
    Enjoy!

Jimmy Plush in the
Tomb of the Martian Pharaoh

Egypt just got worse. It had started out dry, sandy and utterly devoid of worthwhile human culture but somehow it had become something more awful than that—dry, sandy, utterly devoid of worthwhile culture and completely interminable. There hadn't been so much as a band of dirty, scheming Bedouin thieves for over a week now. A week of wandering a desert that hadn't been any good to anybody since Alexander the Great sought to rid it of its negroid cat worshipping savagery.

We brought no food or water as the Sheikh of the City of Brass had told us, we rode no camels, we prayed to no god for help and did not break camp. I was not sure exactly how my stomach could growl so loud when there was nothing but stuffing in it, but it was getting to be unbearable. I considered eating Chang, but he was pretty scrawny and as loyal as he might have been, I somehow didn't think he'd agree to it. I could tell from the ravenous look in his eyes that François was thinking the same thing. The gigantic lumberjack had not eaten since the great feast the djinn had conjured for us.

"My stomach rombles, Monsieur Ploosh. I wurhee for ze revonge alon cannot sate a man forevair. We have wondaired so far…"

Don Pedro patted François on the back.

"Do not panic theñor! It shall not be long before I find the theal that my tattoo matches, the one that the king of the thiudad told us about and we destroy that bathtard Jimmy Plush forever! Theenk of your daughter left at the altar, theenk of my brother! I need only feel my thtomach with hith blood, and you need only do the thame!"

The Spaniard was flamboyant, but a gifted swordsman like he should be. If it hadn't been for him the pirates would surely have gotten us. We learned a lot on that pirate ship, about war, about manhood and about who we could trust. François had thought all Spaniards were weak before they fought side by side, but he'd been proven wrong and he knew that Don Pedro was wise beyond his seven years of age.

François nodded his head gravely and took Chang and me into his heavy, muscular, stinking sweaty arms.

"Ze Spaniard is right! We moost not loose sight of ar goel. Zat will only lead to meesfartune. We moost be veejalant and stroong of weel!"

Veejalant and stroong of weel we were. Starving and dying of thirst, we also were. So, when we saw a colossal, shallow, drinkable lake of sparkling green water we stopped speaking of vengeance, adventure and strength of will and ran toward it. We waded into the shallow water, cupped our hands and drank for a very long time. The water was sweet, there was a hint of lime to it, but it burned a tiny bit like good liquor. Got us a little woozy like good liquor too, but we were mighty thirsty, so we kept drinking. Must have been really good liquor, because in the middle of the lake I hallucinate a gigantic, island sized sea turtle with a concerned look on its huge, sea turtle face.

"You should leave this place," it told me in my liquor water addled head, "you should leave this place before it's too late."

"Do not be stupide, turtle! Zees place ees a good place to be!" Francois replied to the turtle's voice in my head.

"The water eeth deleethious, turtle, you weel not have it all for yourself!" Don Pedro shouted, reprimanding the creature.

"A bad man lives on my back," the turtle explained, "he is worshipped as a god, a bad god. He has tricked the people that live on me and they are not good people anymore. Leave now. While you still can, before the poison in my urine makes you slow."

I shot the turtle in its mansized eye.

"Why did you do that? I was only trying to help you."

Francois swam up to the turtle's eye and began hacking at it with his axe.

"Do not tell us what to do, turtle! And do not hog your precious urine!"

Don Pedro in turn swam up to the eye and started poking it with his saber.

"Yeth! Thith ith the thing to do! We muth not let the turtle trick us out of his magic piss!"

"You are drinking my urine," the turtle calmly explained again, "you are drinking my urine and it is poisonous. If you do not flee as fast as you can, right now, there is going to be trouble."

Chang launched himself at the turtle's forehead, hitting it with a flying kick, then clinging to it, so he could punch it several times.

"You deceive and betray us, giant turtle! Your greed will not be tolerated."

"Alright," the turtle said, it's voice heavy with annoyance, "you can drink all the urine you want, just don't say I didn't warn you."

Chang bowed to the turtle.

"You have fought honorably, giant turtle in my imagination. I honor you with honor."

"Thank you," the turtle replied, his tone patronizing, "I love honor."

Francois laughed heartily.

"Join us, turtle in dreenking your piss! We will get dronk together and we will have merry times!"

"I don't think that's going to happen. You're all going to die soon. I warned you but you've had too much of my urine to drink and you're probably too stupid to listen anyway."

"Keel ze turtle!" Francois resumed his hacking, Don Pedro his stabbing, Chang his karate chops and me my shooting – the buzz from the urine fueling our violence. (I added that line because I feel there needs to be a bit more blatant explanation for all the characters' violence, especially Chang.)

"Actually, the term is zaratan. And stop attacking me. You're all in terrible danger."

Suddenly, Chang collapsed from a blowdart to the neck. Then, Francois collapsed from a blowdart to the neck. And then Don Pedro. As I blacked out from a blowdart to the neck, I could hear the turtle sigh.

"I warned you."

I awakened to typical post blowdart trouble. Chang, Don Pedro, Francois and I were tied to giant beef jerky sticks.

Jackalheaded men were dancing around is in a circle, chanting in some nonsense language. Maybe it was a nonsense language. Maybe it was just French or something. I don't know, all those languages sound like nonsense to me. That was typical post blowdart trouble. The man towering above us, his vast body clothed in the skins of a lot of these jackal-headed men, meant more than typical post blowdart trouble.

This must have been a pretty big turtle if Townsquare Vanzetti could take up residence on its back and start a cult of jackalmen. In the future I would remember to always listen to turtles and not to drink magic pisswater, no matter how good it was or how drunk it got me. All I could do was what I usually did in these situations, create a diversion with some snappy banter while I think of a (usually violent) solution. As I decided to do this, Vanzetti tossed Francois' giant jerky stick into his mouth, swallowing it whole. I started bantering immediately after that.

"So, Vanzetti, you're doing well for yourself. I don't think I know anybody with a cult of jackal people back home."

He chuckled. The turtle shook.

"I can smell the fear on you, Plush. I didn't think teddy bears could sweat."

I could...then I could...maybe...umm...I was drawing a blank. All I could come up with was to banter more.

"So how did you get here? You were dragged into the ocean by half the town."

Vanzetti yanked a nearby palm tree out of the ground, reached into the pocket of his jackalman suit and pulled out a book of giant matches. He lit the palm tree and started to smoke it.

"Yes, Plush, you did me quite the disservice back there. Not only did my congame get revealed to my associates, I had to deal with the harsh facts myself. I hate the Chief Inspector so much! He thwarted me every step of the way for years and to find out it was me was a horrible shock. I spent a year in a coma as I drifted at sea. For six months I came to terms with this horrible realization and then for six months, I engaged in a battle with my other self that raged throughout my psyche. A battle I finally won."

"Good for you," I shot back, "I never liked the Chief Inspector."

"Nobody really did. When I awakened, I found something truly fascinating."

"Your feet?"

Vanzetti chuckled again.

"You wish, Plush, you wish! No, it was a bottle the size of a small ship bobbing alongside me. And there was a message inside. Do you know what it said?"

"Dear Friday, I just don't think it's working out. I've found comfort in the arms of Tarzan of the Apes, yours, Robinson Crusoe." Not the wittiest thing anyone's ever said, but I was under a lot of pressure to keep the conversation going.

Vanzetti didn't appreciate the joke. He plucked Don Pedro's jerky stick from the ground and swallowed him whole. The turtle quaked again with his laughter.

"A tasty morsel, but not very satisfying. Maybe I'm just in the mood for Chinese."

He wanted me to shout out, "no!" – to beg for my chauffeur's life and then for my own. It wasn't something I was going to do. That would be over quickly and besides, giant cannibal mobsters usually could not be talked out of eating people. Still thinking. Still realizing that these ropes are too tight to squirm out of and that it would be hard to jump out of the way as he shoved me down his cavernous throat. Also, violence was out of the question. Situations like this made me see just how often violence actually does get me out of most of my scrapes. When even violence has forsaken you, you've got troubles.

"You trying to scare me by eating my chink? Go ahead and eat the chink, then. I'm not scared, Vanzetti. I'm not scared and I never will be."

"We'll see about that, Plush," he replied. The worst thing about his tone was that it wasn't threatening. He was too sure of himself to need to make threats. I couldn't blame him.

He ate Chang. He ate the faithful chauffeur who I could count on even before the Seven were assembled. I considered violence again, but the opportunity wasn't there. I hated to admit to myself how much I'd needed the goofy, slanty SOB, but I had. And now the Spectacular Seven was down to one. It was one of those times when I felt like I'd always been the least of us.

"You know what that note said, Plush?" he asked.

"You asked me that already."

"And now that you're all alone, I'll tell you. It said to get onto the third zaratan I saw and that it would end up beached in Egypt. And when it was beached in Egypt, I'd get the chance to finish you off once and for all. To kill your friends and get you alone. It was signed Charles Hatbox. In exchange for this information, all he wanted was to make sure my jackalman friends cut out your heart before I swallowed you and sent it to him."

"Then why haven't you cut out my heart?"

"Because I've gotten what I needed from this Hatbox fellow. And when all the fur's been dissolved, I want to be able to taste the meat inside. If there is anything but stuffing."

"Probably isn't. You ought to let me go. I'm not really worth eating."

There was no more banter, Vanzetti picked up the beef jerky stick and swallowed it and me whole. I closed my eyes and prepared for Hell. There was no way a guy like me could expect Heaven.

Hell was something moist and gooey. I was probably in some sort of mud trap. I opened my eyes so I could stare down my demonic tormentors. Apparently, in Hell you got your feet stuck in a chocolate cake the size of an elephant. Apparently in Hell a girl dressed as a squirrel climbed up said cake to help you out of it. Apparently, I was not in Hell. She took my hand to extricate me from the cake and then put me on her back and started the climb down.

"Hang on tight, Mr. Plush. We've been expecting you. Your friends, the sheriff."

"The sheriff of Hell?" I just had to make sure.

"Nah. I don't know if Hell even has a sheriff. Since we're mostly hookers, we're not a very religious people."

"Makes sense."

When we got to the base of the cake a girl dressed in a tight amoeba costume was waiting for me with a bucket of cold water to scrub the cake off of me. As she washed me off, I couldn't help but notice that the cake I'd climbed down from had big double doors on it, as if it were being used as a building. There were several other cakes as well with doors on them and busy Furries went in and out going about whatever business they went about in here.

"Excuse me," I asked the amoeba girl.

"Yes, Mr. Plush?"

"Why does that cake have double doors? Why am I still alive?"

"The sheriff will explain that at city hall."

"City Hall?"

"It's inside the cake."

I didn't even try to ask for an explanation. I don't know why, living a life like mine, I would have expected anybody to have a sensible one. My time as a detective taught me that in the end the solution to every case is that life doesn't make sense and it doesn't have to. A giant mobster can have a belly full of hookers residing in a cake city sometimes. And this giant mobster did. This giant mobster also had a familiar big lumberjack in his stomach, one that set down a large bundle of beef jerky outside of the cake building.

He threw his big, hairy lumberjack arms around me. For once I didn't feel like shooting him in the head for it.

"Monsieur Ploosh! It is un plaisir to see you again!"

"And to see you, Francois. There isn't any way you could explain this to me is there?"

Francois let go so the amoeba girl could return to the business of toweling me off. He did not provide me with the explanation I wanted.

"Done!" said the amoeba girl, toweling me off, "You're ready for your meeting, Mr. Plush."

Francois said nothing. He simply led me into the cake. Gathered around a table made of stale bread were several more Furries of nearly every species imaginable, sultry crayfish, shapely meerkats, buxom voles...Vanzetti had devoured a lot of hookers in his day and variety, for him, must certainly have been the spice of life, adding flavor to each one of the poor unfortunate whores. Also seated around the table were Don Pedro and Chang, who didn't seem any worse for wear. Chang gave a bow.

"It is a relief to see most honored Mister Plush has come out intact."

"Everything but my sanity. Somehow, I've become convinced that I survived being swallowed and now I'm inside a cake meeting with a bunch of Furries and some of my dead compatriots."

"Ah, thenor, Plush! It ith a miracle! We have thurvived because a man of Vanzetti's size takes decades to digest anything!"

"Some miracle. We get to die slow instead of quick?"

A hooker in a crayfish suit laughed.

"Francois told me you were a bit prickly. At least you're not as bad as the rumors around Nero City said you were. You're not going to die in here because Francois and the rest of us have been working on a ladder that leads up to Vanzetti's right eye. All you need to do is go up there, roll it out of the socket and you'll find freedom."

"Sounds disgusting, but I guess that's life."

"Trust me," said the crayfish girl, "it's the only one of the escape routes you'd want to go near."

Francois nodded.

"All of ze rest you could get lost in forever."

"Well, since you put it that way, the eyeball doesn't seem so bad anymore."

A girl in a monitor lizard suit whose bare breasts stuck out through two strategically placed holes entered the cityhall cake, huffing and puffing.

"It's....done."

She collapsed and died on the spot. The hookers gathered around her, recited the Lord's Prayer, then pounced on her, tore off her suit and started to devour her flesh. Had it not been for my time in the police station, I would've been disgusted by the sight of a cake full of prostitutes eating an old friend, but it was in context now. It felt like an act of love. They ate ecstatically, joyfully and tenderly and it seemed as if, in this place, any girl would give herself to feed her friends and colleagues. I was surprised when Francois joined them, until I saw the look in his eyes. He'd fallen in love. With all of these girls. Just like a Frenchman.

Maybe if I were a more softhearted guy like Francois was, I wouldn't be so angry. With a town full of prostitutes that wouldn't be digested for several years head over heels in love with him, who could really blame him for deciding to stay instead of risking death at the hands of the real Jimmy Plush?

The ladder led to a cavern occupied by a white, spongy mass of fat that could only be Vanzetti's eyeball. I shot the thing five times, jumpkicked it, knifehanded it, punched it, kneaded it, elbowed it and shot it five more until it came loose. With another series of kicks, punches and shoves, it rolled out of the socket, letting me once more see the light of day. Chang, Don Pedro and I leapt from the socket down to Vanzetti's enormous shoulders. Before he could shake us off, we zoomed down his arms and hit the ground running pursued by the jackal-headed bastards.

Since it wasn't the first time we'd run from a barrage of spears, we outdistanced the primitive scum and were off the turtle and swimming for our lives in a shallow pool of hallucinogenic zaratan piss in no time. When Plush was dead and I was safe at home, I would have to slow down my life somewhat. When you reach the point where a swim through a pool of turtle piss as spears are being thrown at you is a relief, it's probably time to reevaluate everything. Perhaps I should move out to the country and settle down, do some fishing, sit on my porch whittling tiny wooden canoes. Or larger wooden canoes for if I have to swim for my life in hallucinogenic turtle piss again. Well, we live, we learn, we get wetter, we get wiser. We leave friends behind to live their lives in a mobster full of whores. Boy, back when I was Hatbox all I'd wanted was to tell some stories about cowboys and purple-skinned alien nymphomaniacs.

When we'd outdistanced the oasis and the spears, we came to the legendary Valley of Severed Heads, a place where hills of grinning, stinking decayed skulls leered at travelers, laughed at them and warned them to stay away forever. Having just emerged from a giant eyesocket, being stared at was the last thing I wanted. Their chants of "You or Him", which was not so much painful as painfully obvious didn't make things any more enjoyable. When I'd set out on this quest, I knew it would be either me or him. Any idiot would know that. Didn't see why a bunch of ancient heads should bother to taunt me with it. Too many of the goddamn things to waste ammunition splitting all their skulls, too. I got some consolation from knowing that it couldn't be *that* long before war was declared and Egypt and our boys would bomb the jackal-headed monsters, zaratans and eerie laughing skulls off the map.

At the edge of The Valley of Severed Heads, we were met by a small, pink mechanical man with a head that was pretty similar to a toaster.

"What the hell do you want?" I snapped at the little automaton. It being pink and a foot shorter than I was, I felt pretty tough.

"I have come to greet you."

The three of us waited, heaving large sighs in unison.

"Well? I don't have all day, robot."

"Greetings, earthfolk. You approach the Tomb of the Martian Pharaohs! But beware..."

I shot the tiny robot in the head. For more or less no reason. Well, scratch that. I shot him because something completely unrelated to him annoyed me. Which is a reason. A good enough one for either the real Jimmy Plush or myself to shoot someone for. Besides, it was obvious that we were approaching the Tomb of the Martian Pharoahs. A few feet in the distance was a pyramid made of glowing green space metal with flashing diodes all over it. It sure as hell wasn't Graumann's Chinese Theater. Also couldn't be the Arc de Triomphe. It was a little hot for Paris.

The majestic alien workmanship, the colors, the lights and the scale would have been impressive to somebody who hadn't seen the things I'd seen in my travels and exploits, but it was a bit under whelming. Having just escaped from a giant mobster on the back of a giant turtle I expected a little more than a big green pyramid. The turtle was big and green, Vanzetti was big, so the martians would have to do better than this and some stupid little robot to get me "ooing" and "ahhing" like the tourist I was. The small figure standing at the entrance waiting for us was a start.

The small figure was supposed to be a dead man. Of course, things are always supposed to be other things, so I shouldn't have been surprised. Don Pedro was. The guy was his exact duplicate; seven years old, swarthy, inexplicably mustachioed and inexplicably alive.

"Ramon!" he shouted, "Ramon!"

Don Pedro's twin rushed to him with open arms and embraced him. At least with one arm. The other was reaching for a knife at his side. A knife that he plunged into his brother's back. Don Pedro's face filled with the sting of the blade and the betrayal all at once.

"Ramon! Why?"

"Plush promised me the secrets of the alchemist Alejandro Montoya, the secrets our family has searched for all these centuries. You are a small price to pay for cosmic awareness!"

Don Pedro was tough. He pulled the knife out of his back, backed up and drew his sword, wounded though he had been.

"Thenor Plush, Thenor Chang, the time hath come to take my leave of you! Go, into the pyramid, I will take care of my treacherous brother! En garde, perro!"

Ramon smiled a bloodthirsty smile and drew his blade and a duel that would no doubt be the end of both of them began. A duel that provided me the opportunity to slip into the pyramid. I could have stopped to shoot Ramon in the back but it was the sort of thing that makes Spaniards real sore, so I didn't. I walked through the temple's large, open entry way (which it turns out, had no magic seal to be opened with Don Pedro's tattoo) into a chamber illuminated only by green torches. I didn't like what I saw in there.

There were about fifty of the things. White birds with grilled cheese sandwiches for heads, sandwiches that opened and closed as they squawked out cries of doom, all the while dripping out hot cheese. They were mad, too. When the Professor had told me Martian folklore spoke of grilled cheese sandwich birds, I laughed at him. But nobody was laughing now.

"Go!" Chang screamed at me.

"I can't do that!" I shouted back. "We've already lost too many!"

The birds swooped down at Chang and their cheese burned his face—the flesh starting to sizzle. The grilled cheese sandwich birds were too many for him to take. I took aim, hoping a bullet square in the middle of the flock would scare 'em off.

"*No!*" I don't know how Chang saw through the globs of yellow heat, but he didn't want me to shoot, "you save your bullets! You save your bullets for that bastard, Jimmy Plush!"

"Don't be a fool, Chang!"

"You don't be a fool!" He cut two in half with one chop, "Don Pedro dies for nothing if you don't go on without me. Francois dies for nothing if you don't go on. Most honored Mr. Plush, this is the honorable way."

He was right. Five of the Spectacular Seven were dead now, giving their lives so the archvillain in Charles Hatbox's…in my… body could finally be stopped. Painful as their deaths were, any of them would have done it ten times over if they knew that it would mean the end of that bastard. Also, Chang's face was virtually immune to burning at this point. I felt a great admiration for the Chinaman when I figured out that he had been letting me scald him with hot coffee so his skin would become less heat sensitive in case we got into a situation like this one. More kooky advice from Confucius, most likely, but it worked this time.

I continued deeper into the tomb, following the light of the green torches and the funny scribbles on the wall. They were mostly scribbles that is, except for one. I was taken aback when I saw it. Not the kind of thing you'd expect in a martian tomb. I led the kind of life where there were things to expect from a martian tomb. None of those things were a raised carving of a teddy bear face identical to my own. I felt an inexplicable urge to touch the thing. If you have no good reason to touch a mysterious carving in a martian tomb, it's usually a good idea not to. I should have known this. I did know this. I should have found it strange that I forgot it. But, when one is in a state that would cause them to forget such a rudimentary rule of alien crypt exploration, their will is usually not their own. So, I forgive myself for touching the carving.

There was a flash of light that smelled of strange, exotic space flowers. Though I had never been to space, I knew the name of every component of the sweet smell in the air, from the Saturn meatrose to the hotfudge flytrap of Mercury's fire jungles. The room faded around me, leaving me floating in a starry sky, a sky that offered my mind the name of every one of its millions of stars, a sky that told me that if I survived, I was going to be alright. I asked it what it was that I needed to survive. It replied by grabbing me with a gigantic hand made of stars. The hand reached up and up and up and up and up…

Until it burst through the floor of a sandstone temple not unlike the tomb I had just come from. I was in another long corridor with teddy bear faces carved into the walls with all manner of expressions on them, some laughing, some weeping, some sticking out their tongues, some scowling angrily, some eyeless, some bearing a single eye in the center of their foreheads. As I moved further down the great corridor, my eyes began to play tricks on me. The faces were changing their expressions, smiles becoming frowns and frowns becoming smiles right before my eyes. After all I'd been through, this shouldn't have made me doubt my sanity, but it did. Moreso when I started to hear the sound of laughter.

At the end of the corridor, there was a twenty foot high golden door with a fifteen foot high teddy bear face on it. The face was dead serious until I got closer, and then it smiled widely, after which time it opened, leading me into what must have been an entirely different tomb. This one was bigger inside, taller and full of hundreds of sarcophagi. When I set foot inside they opened, revealing what one would expect from sarcophagi; mummies.

But these were not what I would expect from mummies. Most of the time one suspects mummies to be inanimate, which these mummies were not. Most of the time one does not expect mummies to have neongreen skin and teddy bear heads. Which these mummies did. Also, one does not expect mummies to charge at them en masse, which these mummies did. Apparently, I knew very little about mummies, or else martian mummies were just that different from conventional mummies. I assumed the Chinese fighting arts headstanding pogosnake stance and hoped for the best.

They shuffled at me. From headstanding pogosnake stance, one can execute the upside down whirlwind decapitating batkick, which I did by spinning my legs like helicopter blades and bouncing on my soft, cottony head. My helicopter blade legs took the heads off of three mummies and when I landed and went into a rolling spikeshark roll, I knocked three more of them off balance. And as you probably know, when a foe is on the ground, you can do the on-the-ground implosion chop, which is particularly effective on bodies whose organs have turned to dust. And boy, did those mummies implode easily. There were onions and sawdust everywhere and I was barely getting started.

A few of the mummies revealed that they were capable of shooting blue lasers from their eyes. I was lucky that these mummies were slow and I had been trained in performing acrobatic martial arts maneuvers. I dodged, flipped, decapitation kicked mummies while the laser eyed ones melted their brethren. A year ago, laser eyed mummies would have terrified me, but now? Another kick, another jump. Watch the sawdust and onions fly and then I hardly see myself killing anymore. I see only survival in front of me, only my lack of options. I barely notice when the last of the mummies have either killed each other or been killed by me and I'm alone.

I continued into the tomb and the floor faded away, turning into a river of blue satin. I swam through it, knowing that I could still sink to the bottom and I could still drown, even though it was only fabric. I could still feel and I could still die and I could still love, even though I was only fabric. Those thoughts were not my own. Something on the other end of the river was sending them out to me. But who? Why? I struggled against the fabric current, maneuvered around angry tricycles that tried to nip at my feet, drowned out the calls of mama, mama, mama from baby dolls that swam toward me and then sank to the bottom. There were bigger things ahead.

Literally.

When I emerged from the river, dripping with satin, I found myself in a giant chamber with walls made of tin cowboys shooting capguns back and forth at one another. In the center of the room was a smiling teddy bear face glowing green like many of the other smiling teddy bear faces and this one was every bit as seductive, every bit as off kilter. In a language of humming martian vibrations that I shouldn't have been able to understand, it told me to go to it and kneel there for three days. When a green glowing sigil on the floor tells you to kneel for three days, you do it.

So, I went to the sigil and I knelt down. The cowboys on the walls turned their capguns away from each other and pointed them at me, continuously pelting me with hot, smelly smoky capgun fire. I should have been distracted by taking bullets from thousands of tiny, belligerent tin cowboys, but I wasn't. I should have been distracted by thoughts of the real Jimmy Plush grabbing the lingam and making this world his, but I wasn't. I thought only of kneeling and glowing.

This place was having a strange effect on me.

After the third day, a fifty foot high naked green woman appeared. I felt the stirring of a phantom erection, a Charles Hatbox erection. She was a real hot fifty foot tomato, legs, hips, waist, bosom made as well as they'd ever been. It didn't bother me that the hair around her pussy was made up of smiling teddy bear faces, it didn't bother me that instead of nipples she had two teddy bear heads. It didn't bother me that her head was that of a green, mouthless teddy bear. I felt a stirring in me, I felt like a man again in her presence.

Her left teddy bear nipple opened its mouth. It spoke in a commanding womanly voice, a voice like a gossamer hatchet.

"Welcome, Charles Hatbox."

"Thank you," I replied, bowing down and kissing her left foot. Like most of my actions of late, I did not know at all why I did so.

The right nipple spoke up next. Its voice was a softer, breathier version of the same voice.

"Welcome Hieronymous James Plush."

"Thank you." I bowed down and kissed her right foot. Hot and cold feelings fought for dominion over my body. I liked these new stirrings of pleasure and the slight feeling of divine serenity, but I was not happy about being driven to actions I didn't understand. If I was going to lose control of myself, I at least wanted to be able to blame it on too much gin.

"You are hungry," said the left nipple.

"He is desperately lacking in nourishment," the right continued.

"If he wishes to live he must feed," said the left.

"I concur."

She lowered one of her great big mitts and I climbed on and

was brought from mitt to tit, brought up to her left breast.

"Open wide, Charles Hatbox and be fed."

I opened my mouth and the nipple opened its mouth. It spat green martian milk into my opened mouth. Delicious green martian milk. I floated in the air, my soul bathed in starlight, my mind opened as far as a French girl's legs and I saw Charles Hatbox born, Charles Hatbox suckled, Charles Hatbox riding a tricycle, Charles Hatbox dressed as a cowboy firing a capgun, Charles Hatbox opening a Christmas gift. A small, familiar Christmas gift. A Christmas gift that looked at me from the mirror every damned, accursed day since…he…I…he named the bear Jimmy Plush. His mother sewed a tiny fedora. Hatbox brought it everywhere, they pretended to solve mysteries in the livingroom and in his backyard. It was only the size of a regular teddy bear, but it was sure as hell Jimmy Plush. What could this have meant? Hatbox throwing the bear out. Hatbox in school, hiding, slinking, unknown and mediocre. Hatbox writing the novel nobody wanted. Hatbox trying to make some money playing cards, winning a couple poker games. Hatbox losing poker games. Hatbox getting rejected. Hatbox being shot down by girl after girl after girl and magazine after magazine. Hatbox getting into hot water with Halperin, Hatbox meeting Jimmy Plush, feeling a faint glimmer of recognition and thinking he was worth trusting. Hatbox making the last mistake I would make as Hatbox. Hatbox slipping away.

"Why are you giving this back?" I asked, tears dampening my fur, "I don't want this as me. I want this as Hatbox. I want to be Hatbox again, so I'm going to get the lingam and I'm going to get myself back. Stop torturing me!"

"This is not torture," said the right breast, "we are imparting wisdom. Wisdom that you will end up needing."

"What if I don't want it?"

"You've passed the point at which it would have been your choice. And I am truly sorry for that."

The hand grabbed me again and raised me to the right breast.

"Eat up, Hieronymous James Plush and be nourished."

Lightness. Stars. Dizziness. A child playing detective. A child dragging me downstairs. A child holding me at night, every night. Holding back words because I'm not permitted to say them. Holding back anger at being left out in the mud and then being violently scrubbed. Garbage in an alley, I stand up and I scream. I begin to grow up, standing three feet high, unafraid of language, angry, angry, angry. A gun, a fedora, a bottle of gin, answering questions for any who needed them answered. Making short work of anyone who got in the way. Awful things. Lies, crooked cases, double crosses. Deviant sex, unnecessary violence, an abused chauffeur and nobody to answer to but me. And why should I answer to anybody? I'm the baddest teddy bear in town. The others get dragged downstairs, covered in mud, abandoned, not me. I'm nobody's toy. This city is my plaything. The world is my plaything and it will be mine. A greenskinned monk, a strange book, a chance to get back at the man I hated most. Almost too easy. But of course it was. Wasn't anybody better than Jimmy Plush.

This time I threw up the milk. I couldn't stand the things that were inside of Jimmy Plush. There was no reason anybody should have to. Made me want to leave right away so I could get to killing the bastard and making sure only Hatbox remained.

"Thanks, ma'am…ladies? Whatever I call you. I've made my decision now. Hatbox lives and Plush dies today. No need the world should have to deal with that teddybastard."

"You're unarmed," said the left breast.

"Very risky."

"You need a weapon."

I shook my head.

"I only need my hands to bring him down."

The right breast contradicted me.

"He knows what you know. He knows how you fight and he has a fullgrown man's body to fight with."

"He is a clever and dangerous opponent."

"I cannot let you take him on unarmed."

A ladder of doll arms extended down from her sex.

"Grab hold of the arms."

"Climb the ladder."

"Claim your gifts."

"Claim your power."

"Become the man who will survive."

"Or the bear."

"Or the bear, yes, or the bear."

The giant hand set me down at her feet again.

"Go ahead, climb into my womb."

I had more reason to trust her than I had most people. As much pain she might have caused, she caused it by telling the truth which is something I didn't tell myself very often. My commitment to finding it for others was usually a professional necessity and most of the time when I did, it was because I'd end up finding my way back to somebody's door that I already felt was worth kicking down. She had filled me with serenity and fear and hope and confusion and clarity. I climbed the doll arms knowing that ahead would probably be more of this. At the top, green Plush lips parted and I was once again someplace else.

But where? It looked like Nero City but everything was sort of a silhouette. Silhouette buildings, silhouette cars, silhouette whores against silhouette lampposts, silhouette mothers with silhouette strollers with silhouette babies inside them. I felt tall, fleshy and sad. I knew this feeling. This was Charles Hatbox. I was Hatbox again, walking down these shadow streets. I opened up my wallet as I approached a silhouette girl's lamppost.

"How much for a good time?"

She put her hand on her chin.

'Bssspppppspsspsssbsssp," she whispered.

"Excuse me?"

"Bssssppssssspbsbbbssbbbsppsppp," she whispered.

"Can you speak louder."

"Sppppsspspspspsspspppspspspspsppppspspspsp, sppbbspsspbh, shhhhspsspsp," she replied, no louder than before.

Suddenly, a great shadow loomed behind her, holding up a big shadowy sledgehammer. I tried to shout "look out", but the words never left my mouth. I reached into my pocket for my gun but found only a tunafish sandwich and a copy of Tarzan of the Apes. The sledgehammer came down, pounding her into inky pulp, but I didn't care. I walked away from the crime scene to find a game of three card monte.

On that, I fared a bit better. There was a shadow man with a shadowy table but the cards on it were real. I laid down five dollars. He shuffled them around, then told me with a gesture to pick one. I picked the one in the middle. Had to be the one. There was a smiling teddy bear face on it. An arrogant, patronizing, evil smiling teddy bear face. I laid down another five and we played the game again. The one on the left. Had to be the one on the left. Smiling teddy bear face. Five dollars. One in the middle. Smiling teddy bear face. Five dollars. One on the left. Smiling teddy bear face. Five dollars five dollars five dollars teddy bear…I shook myself from inside, told me to end this. As I fought for control, I…Hatbox…I dropped more and more money. I was starting to hear tiny laughter from the teddy bear on the card. At last, I managed to pull away from the three card monte game, running down the black identical streets to find my home.

In the middle of a shadowy slum was a perfectly solid tenement which I knew I resided at. I did not feel proud to reside here but don't remember caring much that I had at one point. I walked past many identical dingy apartments, until I came to my dingy apartment. A skinny Dalmatian ceased pondering his empty dish to approach me.

"You've got a lot of nerve, you worthless shit."

"Excuse me?"

"Jimmy Plush killed me. Sent the meat to your girlfriend. She sold it to Halperin."

"I'm really sorry, dog," was all I could think to say.

"Doesn't bring me back, does it?"

There was a cowboy sitting on my couch, dribbling blood out of his mouth. His face was more hollow than the dalmatian's, he looked like he hadn't eaten in weeks.

He tried to stand up, but ended up rolling onto the floor, where he started crawling toward me.

"Feed me! You son of a bitch! Feed me! Feed me!" the cowboy shrieked. I backed away, seeing no option but to hide in the tiny bedroom. I knew I had nothing for the dog or the cowboy and I knew that they had every right to blame me for the state they were in.

I locked the bedroom door, thinking I can breathe easy, but heard a breathy feminine voice beg.

"Feed me, feed me, feed me, oh god, feed me…"

Lying on the bed dying was a purple skinned alien princess, skeletal and demanding, her spacebreasts all the more big, round and obscene compared to her tiny, dying body. She crawled off the bed and onto the floor to pursue me. I had to open the door again, to get away from her, even if it meant having to deal with the cowboy and the dog. I ran for the front door, kicking clawlike starving hands and grasping paws away from me as they closed in.

Kicking them aside, I reached the hallway and knocked on my neighbor's door for help. A starving man in a spacesuit answered, I could barely see his face since his helmet's faceplate was splattered and obscured with blood. He reached out to me, mumbling into his helmet. I knew he wanted to be fed. These were my unwanted children, the creations of my hack imagination (and my dog) having to live only on the meager hopes of the worst pulp writer who ever lived. I was a man who could not even dream right.

They were closing in on me now, the only place that I could possibly think to hide was in the elevator. I got in and they did not even try to follow. On the wall of the elevator, there was one big button: it was a green teddy bear's face, glowing and whispering secrets with its vibrations. I pressed it and as it should have, the elevator started to rise and rise and rise…

The elevator door opened into a green fleshy cave. I was Jimmy Plush again. Or I was Hatbox-Plush. Whatever. I was no longer Charles Hatbox. It felt like a relief for once. I'd forgotten what my life had been like. Spending time as a crime-solving teddy bear who was hated all over town could do that to a guy. All the weak heroes, all the vulnerable fantasies and all the lost possibilities hadn't occurred to me. Why should they have? Life was as bad as it could get. Dodging bullets, returning fire, fistfights with gangsters and freaks, journeys into magical tombs weren't signs of success by any measure of the word. It didn't matter, did it? I'd be a man again. Dammit. This was so confusing. I screamed at the top of my little teddy bear lungs. If I had lungs. Somebody screamed back.

"Not so goddamn loud!" said a voice from deeper in the cavern.

"Hello?" I shouted.

A short, squat green man in a monk's robe, a man I'd seen when the right breast showed me Jimmy Plush's life, hobbled in on a cane.

"You? Hmm. I'd been expecting the other one."

"He's probably off stealing the lingam."

The green monk shrugged.

"I don't know."

Since I hadn't expected a tiny green monk here in the womb of the giant teddy bear goddess, I decided I should probably find out what he was doing here.

"Who are you and what are you doing here?"

He looked at me as if it were a ridiculous thing to ask, as if any man on the street could answer the question for him.

"It should be obvious."

"Maybe I'm slow. Tell me."

"I'm the high scholarpriest of the Martian Teddy Bear Goddess, Sekharun."

Sekharun, huh? Sounded good.

"Pretty name."

The scholarpriest laughed.

"Beyond that. In our language it means Arbiter of Transcendant Joys."

"Your language being Martian?"

"Yes. The task that brings me joy is to guard the treasures that are supposed to be here."

"So you guard the lingam?"

"No, sometimes I go to the outside world to spread stories of the lingam and the glories of Mars, but I do not guard the lingam. It's not supposed to be here. I only guard treasure that's supposed to be here. The computosphinx guards the lingam. Only the wisest of men may pass without being torn to shreds by its wrath."

"So what treasure do you guard?"

He made a face.

"Whatever's supposed to be here."

As he said this, a large golden chest appeared. He examined it for a couple of seconds, mumbled something to himself then sat down and entered a deep meditative trance for a minute.

"This is yours," he said upon awakening.

"Alright. Is there something I need to do?"

"Why would there be something you need to do? Didn't I say it's yours?"

"But aren't you supposed to guard the treasure that's supposed to be here?"

"Why should I guard it? It's yours."

I still couldn't help but think that this monk was not particularly good at guarding things. But, that didn't matter. I opened up the chest. There was a curved sword, some sort of zapgun and a pair of grey, wool pants inside.

It was a nice gesture on the part of the goddess, but I felt sort of lost again.

"What are these?"

The monk looked inside the chest.

"Well, from the looks of things, an enchanted scimitar sacred to Osiris, a Martian disintegrator ray and a pair of wool trousers. All things you need. Very good gifts."

He was right about that. If anybody needed a Martian disintegrator ray, it was me. The sword looked expensive, too. Still wasn't sure about the pants. I never wore pants because I never had anything to…I felt a heaviness between my legs. A familiar but foreign heaviness. A happy new heaviness that made me feel complete. I cried tears of joy when I discovered that from now on, I would need to wear pants and barring the vaults of particularly depraved collectors, I was the world's first anatomically correct three foot tall teddy bear.

"See," said the monk, "very good gifts. The goddess provides. You should put on those pants."

I did. Gladly. They were a perfect fit. Not that I would expect pants manifested by the cosmos to be anything but. Magic sword, raygun, manhood. I felt ready for just about anything. I wasn't even bothered by the giant hand that reached through the soft, cushiony green…oh. Considering how I'd come in, I should have known what this cavern was. The knowledge was beautiful and disturbing at the same time. I sat down in the palm of the hand and let it lower me back down through the womb, which it did, but it set me down somewhere else entirely.

Another one of those big sandstone chambers. Boy was I getting tired of big sandstone chambers. You'd think Martians would be more creative. Apparently, they thought the best thing Earth had to offer was sandstone. Well, they had to be fond of sand anyway to decide that Egypt was the best place to build their tombs. In this particular sandstone room, I found something unique: bits of shattered metal wings, shattered metallic lion parts and some high tech space teddy bear's head. Its mouth opened and closed, repeating "Why? Why? Why?"

This must once have been the fierce computosphinx—then Jimmy Plush was already headed for the lingam chamber. I drew the sword and raygun and ran ahead.

The chamber beyond the computosphinx glowed gold, a welcome change from sandstone and in here were statues of gods I'd heard of before, gods without teddybear heads, a god with a crocodile head, a goddess with a lion head and a tall, kingly god. Would have been a beautiful place if it wasn't for Jimmy Plush in the body of Charles Hatbox with a huge, mummified penis in his hand. Not something I wanted to see. Just plain disturbing first of all and secondly, it meant that Plush had the artifact he wanted. For once I didn't waste any time with banter. I took aim with the Martian disintegrator and hoped it disintegrated teddy bear bastards in pulp writer bodies. It let out a green laser beam that hit Plush square in what used to be my chest.

And nothing happened.

"Damn cheap space garbage…" I mumbled.

"The disintegrator's fine, Hatbox," said Plush, "but you've forgotten that when we were in Atlantis, I was showered in magical radiation, the kind of magical radiation that would repel Martian lasers. Or have you forgotten that Atlantis was founded by aliens of Venusian extraction?"

Damn. Professor Svenson would have known that. I wish I could've saved him from those rhinos.

"Doesn't matter. I'll find some way to kill you, Plush."

He laughed contemptuously.

"With that Martian pigsticker of yours?"

He reached into his trenchcoat and pulled out a spiky, red sword.

"This sword is forged of adamantine coral by Atlantis' finest swordsmith."

There was only one thing I could say in response to that.

"En garde, you bastard!"

I lunged with the scimitar and he parried. I went in for a punch with my offhand only to find there was a knife in his. He thrust into my palm, spilling some stuffing. He laughed again, a haughty Errol Flynn laugh that should never have come out of Charles Hatbox's mouth.

"Ha! First blood."

Since my palm was already cut and in pain, I really didn't have anything to lose from grabbing the blade, nothing but more cotton. It was worth it to take hold of the knife and toss him over my shoulder using the Chinese fighting arts. He flew a couple feet, hit the ground and I'm sure spilled a little blood of his own. I turned just in time to avoid getting stabbed in the back as he got to his feet, surprised to find that there was only a small bump on his head. Guy must have really known how to fall.

"I'm impressed. Nice work…for a teddy bear!" He surprised me with a particularly aggressive lunge, one I almost couldn't parry. He surprised me again with a kick in the chest. I had less luck with the kick than with the lunge and flew back a few feet. I was dazed, so by the time I got to my feet he had closed the distance and he was ready for me. He smiled a smile I had never known my former face was capable of. Damn. I hope I never looked that vile when I smiled at people.

"This is the end, Plush. I've brought you here to finish you off, to cut out my own heart so I can work the lingam. I couldn't very well cut out my heart when it was in *my* body could I? And there were so many things you'd done to me that needed paying back. Dragging me through the mud, tossing me down the stairs…this is going to hurt so much worse than getting tossed down stairs…"

I closed my eyes expecting decapitation, feeling that this must surely be the end of the line. I opened them when I heard a "swoosh" and a "thud", to see that the chauffeur I had thought dead had not been killed by the grilled cheese sandwich birds and had come out of nowhere to knock Jimmy Plush to the ground with a flying kick.

"Dishonorable Mister Plush, the time has come for revenge!"

"I couldn't agree more," said Plush, rising to his feet.

The Chinaman leapt at Plush, preparing to kick his head clean off but it was not to be. Plush was quick on the draw with his Atlantean Disemboweler pistol, the pistol he had fired at Captain Von Frankenstein when the undead pirate had decided that Plush was too vile even for him to side with. I did not close my eyes as the gun ripped Chang's intestines out of his body. The least I could do was witness his grisly death.

In the next few moments, three factors worked against Plush: first of all, Atlantean Disemboweler pistols only carry two shots, second of all, his hatred of the Chinese made the whole spectacle mesmerizing and hilarious to him and third of all, I was small fast and angry. Scimitar drawn, I leapt at the laughing sadist, slicing into his legs. He bled. He stumbled. I hacked. He bled. He stumbled. I hacked. He hit the floor. I jumped on his stomach.

"So you going to cut my heart out to wish for your own body back?" he laughed hysterically, "Then I've still won. I've made you sacrifice lives, take bullets, do things a man should never have to do just so you can resume being your original crummy self instead of having a chance at the earth and all of its splendors, or wishing for harems of beautiful women or…"

I sliced his throat to shut him up. He was right. And hell, from all I'd learned and all I'd done, I figured out it meant something to be Jimmy Plush. I had my gun, I had my wits and I had a few inches where a man needs to have 'em. No point asking for the world. I had killed the bastard Jimmy Plush and the bastard Charles Hatbox in one stroke of my sword and walked out of the temple as the one, the only, the new and improved heroic Jimmy Plush. Not too bad of a thing to be.

I returned to the only place I really knew, in spite of hating it. It was different, though. Where once I saw only filth, disease and stupidity, now I saw potential. Towns, countries, they're like people themselves, they don't turn good or bad overnight, they get better or they get worse, they do one evil thing or one good thing at a time, they lose people, they kill people they get dragged downstairs or brought in by cops that cut off limbs. It hurt to look at the driverless limo outside my office but I couldn't stop staring. The best man I knew was dead.

If I'd been able to pay attention, I would have seen the smelly, Chinese brutes sneaking up behind me to stuff me in a sack. But I wasn't able to pay attention and they got the drop on me because of it. I didn't mind being stuffed in a sack that much anyway. I'd been through worse and if I felt like getting out of the sack, I had a scimitar and a martian disintegrator inside my coat. I waited.

When they removed me from the sack, I was rewarded by the sight of a pale, angry, Chinese woman. She'd be kind of a looker if she wasn't Chinese, and if she wasn't my dead chauffeur's estranged wife taking revenge for his death and the humiliation he'd suffered at the hands of both me and the real Jimmy Plush. The long, razor sharp fingernails and the gang of Chinese thugs didn't do much for her appeal either.

"Tear him apart!" she ordered them, "Let him die before my eyes!"

There were about twenty of 'em, real big for Chinese, a couple of eunuchs among them that towered over the others. A fella without a martian disintegrator would worry. I fired on the brutes, hoping to sizzle them with hot green death, but failing to remember that the Chinese are descended from the Venusians that colonized Atlantis, so were genetically immune to martian disintegrators, though unfortunately for Chang, not to the disembowelers their species used. Failing to blast my assailants, I drew the scimitar, outmaneuvering them with my agility and knowledge of the fighting arts. Big as these guys were, I made short work of them and headed for the door.

"Where are you going, coward?" Chang's wife shouted at me.

"I'm turning my back on you and walking away." I knew as I said it that it wouldn't be that simple. She practically flew across the room to block the door. I didn't think anybody could move that quick.

"My husband is dead because of you! I am not leaving until I've ripped everything out from inside of you!" She showed she was going to make good on her threat by attempting a good old fashioned open palmed heartripper. I saw it coming, so I could block it.

"I'm not the man you think I am. I did take your husband to his doom but I'm…"

She intended to shut me up with a gilded battleaxe fist. It worked, for a second, my concentration focused on a crawling banana slug sweep, which she deftly dodged, but I was determined to say my peace.

"There was another man who was me before I was. He…"

"Enough of your lies!" She launched into the decapitating batkick. I ducked, readying myself to spikeshark roll when she landed. We exchanged meaningless blow after meaningless blow after meaningless blow, counterattack after counterattack, me wanting nothing more than to make her stop attacking, her wanting nothing more than to keep it up until I was dead. We fought like this for longer than I thought I could fight anyone and god help me, I started to really feel the new equipment. She wasn't just pretty for a Chinese woman, she was pretty for a woman.

We sat down and caught our breath.

"We both lost everything. The man who killed your husband is an associate of the man who killed my girlfriend and my fiancée. He ruined my life and I have to start over from nothin'. Did the same to you."

There was understanding and sympathy in her sweet shadowy eyes.

"You don't seem like the man my husband wrote home about. You seem sad and good and honest."

"I'm tryin'."

"I could have been like my husband," she said, tears flowing down her cheek, "but I'm impatient. I have hate in my heart. I ran my gang in China and he came here to be an honest man."

"It's hard to be the kind of man your husband was."

She put her hand on my thigh to comfort me and was surprised by what she found. As I said, I'd been getting very excited. She pulled off her kimono, opened up my pants and for the first time in I don't know how long, I was inside a woman, part of her, moving in her and feeling something, as if, for once, there was more in me than stuffing and pain. As she held me close, I thought again about what it meant to be Jimmy Plush. I was soft, warm, a thing to make people feel secure and like they live in a good enough world.

"I'll be back," I told her, "I've got some business."

"You'd better be," she said, and meant it.

I agree that storming into J.L Wong's and martian disintegrating Skinny and Johnny was the kind of thing the first Jimmy Plush would have done but the new, improved Jimmy Plush wasn't gonna be a saint just because the last one was a bastard. That would be letting him win. I was through living my life by standards set for and by other people. Anybody who's read a pulp novel before knows that heroic and merciful ain't synonymous.

Which is why what I did after kicking in the door to Vic Halperin's office surprised me.

It was quick and pathetic. I kicked in the door. He reached for his gun. I disintegrated it. He attempted a very respectable jumpkick. I responded with a much more respectable sidestep. He hit the floor hard. I pointed the disintegrator at his head. He started begging for his life.

"What do you want, Plush? Please, anything!"

I looked past the real Jimmy Plush and I looked past Charles Hatbox and I looked into myself.

"First of all, you're out of the pimp business."

He nodded in agreement.

"Fine. Will that be all?"

I shook my head.

"How's your driving?"

ABOUT THE AUTHOR

GARRETT COOK is an author of Bizarro and horror fiction that he has publicly referred to as Neopulp Expressionism and Chainsaw Noir. He hopes to make these phrases mean as much as possible. He enjoys hats, cult cinema,comics and cooking. This is his first book with Eraserhead Press, but not his first book ever. To find out more about him and read free fiction and movie reviews go to http://chainsawnoir.wordpress.com

Bizarro books

CATALOG   SPRING 2011

Bizarro Books publishes under the following imprints:

www.rawdogscreamingpress.com

www.eraserheadpress.com

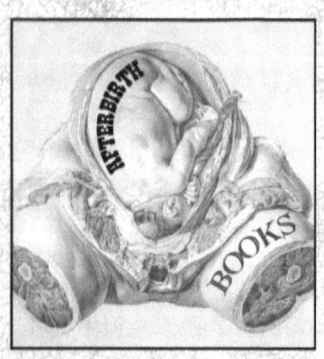

www.afterbirthbooks.com

www.swallowdownpress.com

For all your Bizarro needs visit:

WWW.BIZARROCENTRAL.COM

Introduce yourselves to the bizarro fiction genre and all of its authors with the Bizarro Starter Kit series. Each volume features short novels and short stories by ten of the leading bizarro authors, designed to give you a perfect sampling of the genre for only $10.

BB-0X1
"The Bizarro Starter Kit"
(Orange)
Featuring D. Harlan Wilson, Carlton Mellick III, Jeremy Robert Johnson, Kevin L Donihe, Gina Ranalli, Andre Duza, Vincent W. Sakowski, Steve Beard, John Edward Lawson, and Bruce Taylor.
236 pages $10

BB-0X2
"The Bizarro Starter Kit"
(Blue)
Featuring Ray Fracalossy, Jeremy C. Shipp, Jordan Krall, Mykle Hansen, Andersen Prunty, Eckhard Gerdes, Bradley Sands, Steve Aylett, Christian TeBordo, and Tony Rauch. **244 pages $10**

BB-0X2
"The Bizarro Starter Kit"
(Purple)
Featuring Russell Edson, Athena Villaverde, David Agranoff, Matthew Revert, Andrew Goldfarb, Jeff Burk, Garrett Cook, Kris Saknussemm, Cody Goodfellow, and Cameron Pierce **264 pages $10**

BB-001 "The Kafka Effekt" D. Harlan Wilson - A collection of forty-four irreal short stories loosely written in the vein of Franz Kafka, with more than a pinch of William S. Burroughs sprinkled on top. **211 pages $14**

BB-002 "Satan Burger" Carlton Mellick III - The cult novel that put Carlton Mellick III on the map ... Six punks get jobs at a fast food restaurant owned by the devil in a city violently overpopulated by surreal alien cultures. **236 pages $14**

BB-003 "Some Things Are Better Left Unplugged" Vincent Sakwoski - Join The Man and his Nemesis, the obese tabby, for a nightmare roller coaster ride into this postmodern fantasy. **152 pages $10**

BB-004 "Shall We Gather At the Garden?" Kevin L Donihe - Donihe's Debut novel. Midgets take over the world, The Church of Lionel Richie vs. The Church of the Byrds, plant porn and more! **244 pages $14**

BB-005 "Razor Wire Pubic Hair" Carlton Mellick III - A genderless humandildo is purchased by a razor dominatrix and brought into her nightmarish world of bizarre sex and mutilation.   **176 pages $11**

BB-006 "Stranger on the Loose" D. Harlan Wilson - The fiction of Wilson's 2nd collection is planted in the soil of normalcy, but what grows out of that soil is a dark, witty, otherworldly jungle... **228 pages $14**

BB-007 "The Baby Jesus Butt Plug" Carlton Mellick III - Using clones of the Baby Jesus for anal sex will be the hip sex fetish of the future. **92 pages $10**

BB-008 "Fishyfleshed" Carlton Mellick III - The world of the past is an illogical flatland lacking in dimension and color, a sick-scape of crispy squid people wandering the desert for no apparent reason. **260 pages $14**

BB-009 "Dead Bitch Army" Andre Duza - Step into a world filled with racist teenagers, cannibals, 100 warped Uncle Sams, automobiles with razor-sharp teeth, living graffiti, and a pissed-off zombie bitch out for revenge. **344 pages $16**

BB-010 "The Menstruating Mall" Carlton Mellick III - "The Breakfast Club meets Chopping Mall as directed by David Lynch." - Brian Keene **212 pages $12**

BB-011 "Angel Dust Apocalypse" Jeremy Robert Johnson - Meth-heads, man-made monsters, and murderous Neo-Nazis. "Seriously amazing short stories..." - Chuck Palahniuk, author of Fight Club **184 pages $11**

BB-012 "Ocean of Lard" Kevin L Donihe / Carlton Mellick III - A parody of those old Choose Your Own Adventure kid's books about some very odd pirates sailing on a sea made of animal fat. **176 pages $12**

BB-015 "Foop!" Chris Genoa - Strange happenings are going on at Dactyl, Inc, the world's first and only time travel tourism company. "A surreal pie in the face!" - Christopher Moore **300 pages $14**

BB-020 "Punk Land" Carlton Mellick III - In the punk version of Heaven, the anarchist utopia is threatened by corporate fascism and only Goblin, Mortician's sperm, and a blue-mohawked female assassin named Shark Girl can stop them. **284 pages $15**

BB-021 "Pseudo-City" D. Harlan Wilson - Pseudo-City exposes what waits in the bathroom stall, under the manhole cover and in the corporate boardroom, all in a way that can only be described as mind-bogglingly irreal. **220 pages $16**

BB-023 "Sex and Death In Television Town" Carlton Mellick III - In the old west, a gang of hermaphrodite gunslingers take refuge from a demon plague in Telos: a town where its citizens have televisions instead of heads. **184 pages $12**

BB-027 "Siren Promised" Jeremy Robert Johnson & Alan M Clark - Nominated for the Bram Stoker Award. A potent mix of bad drugs, bad dreams, brutal bad guys, and surreal/incredible art by Alan M. Clark. **190 pages $13**

BB-030 "Grape City" Kevin L. Donihe - More Donihe-style comedic bizarro about a demon named Charles who is forced to work a minimum wage job on Earth after Hell goes out of business. **108 pages $10**

BB-031"Sea of the Patchwork Cats" Carlton Mellick III - A quiet dreamlike tale set in the ashes of the human race. For Mellick enthusiasts who also adore The Twilight Zone. **112 pages $10**

BB-032 "Extinction Journals" Jeremy Robert Johnson - An uncanny voyage across a newly nuclear America where one man must confront the problems associated with loneliness, insane dieties, radiation, love, and an ever-evolving cockroach suit with a mind of its own. **104 pages $10**

BB-034 "The Greatest Fucking Moment in Sports" Kevin L. Donihe - In the tradition of the surreal anti-sitcom Get A Life comes a tale of triumph and agape love from the master of comedic bizarro. **108 pages $10**

BB-035 "The Troublesome Amputee" John Edward Lawson - Disturbing verse from a man who truly believes nothing is sacred and intends to prove it. **104 pages $9**

BB-037 "The Haunted Vagina" Carlton Mellick III - It's difficult to love a woman whose vagina is a gateway to the world of the dead. **132 pages $10**

BB-042 "Teeth and Tongue Landscape" Carlton Mellick III - On a planet made out of meat, a socially-obsessive monophobic man tries to find his place amongst the strange creatures and communities that he comes across. **110 pages $10**

BB-043 **"War Slut" Carlton Mellick III** - Part "1984," part "Waiting for Go-dot," and part action horror video game adaptation of John Carpenter's "The Thing." **116 pages $10**

BB-045 **"Dr. Identity" D. Harlan Wilson** - Follow the Dystopian Duo on a killing spree of epic proportions through the irreal postcapitalist city of Bliptown where time ticks sideways, artificial Bug-Eyed Monsters punish citizens for consumer-capitalist lethargy, and ultraviolence is as essential as a daily multivitamin. **208 pages $15**

BB-047 **"Sausagey Santa" Carlton Mellick III** - A bizarro Christmas tale featuring Santa as a piratey mutant with a body made of sausages. 124 pages $10

BB-048 **"Misadventures in a Thumbnail Universe" Vincent Sakowski** - Dive deep into the surreal and satirical realms of neo-classical Blender Fiction, filled with television shoes and flesh-filled skies. **120 pages $10**

BB-049 **"Vacation" Jeremy C. Shipp** - Blueblood Bernard Johnson left his boring life behind to go on The Vacation, a year-long corporate sponsored odyssey. But instead of seeing the world, Bernard is captured by terrorists, becomes a key figure in secret drug wars, and, worse, doesn't once miss his secure American Dream. **160 pages $14**

BB-053 **"Ballad of a Slow Poisoner" Andrew Goldfarb** Millford Mutter-wurst sat down on a Tuesday to take his afternoon tea, and made the unpleasant discovery that his elbows were becoming flatter. **128 pages $10**

BB-055 **"Help! A Bear is Eating Me" Mykle Hansen** - The bizarro, heart-warming, magical tale of poor planning, hubris and severe blood loss... **150 pages $11**

BB-056 **"Piecemeal June" Jordan Krall** - A man falls in love with a living sex doll, but with love comes danger when her creator comes after her with crab-squid assassins. **90 pages $9**

BB-058 **"The Overwhelming Urge" Andersen Prunty** - A collection of bizarro tales by Andersen Prunty. **150 pages $11**

BB-059 **"Adolf in Wonderland" Carlton Mellick III** - A dreamlike adventure that takes a young descendant of Adolf Hitler's design and sends him down the rabbit hole into a world of imperfection and disorder. **180 pages $11**

BB-061 **"Ultra Fuckers" Carlton Mellick III** - Absurdist suburban horror about a couple who enter an upper middle class gated community but can't find their way out. **108 pages $9**

BB-062 **"House of Houses" Kevin L. Donihe** - An odd man wants to marry his house. Unfortunately, all of the houses in the world collapse at the same time in the Great House Holocaust. Now he must travel to House Heaven to find his departed fiancee. **172 pages $11**

BB-064 **"Squid Pulp Blues" Jordan Krall** - In these three bizarro-noir novellas, the reader is thrown into a world of murderers, drugs made from squid parts, deformed gun-toting veterans, and a mischievous apocalyptic donkey. **204 pages $12**

BB-065 **"Jack and Mr. Grin" Andersen Prunty** - "When Mr. Grin calls you can hear a smile in his voice. Not a warm and friendly smile, but the kind that seizes your spine in fear. You don't need to pay your phone bill to hear it. That smile is in every line of Prunty's prose." - Tom Bradley. **208 pages $12**

BB-066 **"Cybernetrix" Carlton Mellick III** - What would you do if your normal everyday world was slowly mutating into the video game world from Tron? **212 pages $12**

BB-072 **"Zerostrata" Andersen Prunty** - Hansel Nothing lives in a tree house, suffers from memory loss, has a very eccentric family, and falls in love with a woman who runs naked through the woods every night. **144 pages $11**

BB-073 **"The Egg Man" Carlton Mellick III -** It is a world where humans reproduce like insects. Children are the property of corporations, and having an enormous ten-foot brain implanted into your skull is a grotesque sexual fetish. Mellick's industrial urban dystopia is one of his darkest and grittiest to date. **184 pages $11**

BB-074 **"Shark Hunting in Paradise Garden" Cameron Pierce -** A group of strange humanoid religious fanatics travel back in time to the Garden of Eden to discover it is invested with hundreds of giant flying maneating sharks. **150 pages $10**

BB-075 **"Apeshit" Carlton Mellick III -** Friday the 13th meets Visitor Q. Six hipster teens go to a cabin in the woods inhabited by a deformed killer. An incredibly fucked-up parody of B-horror movies with a bizarro slant. **192 pages $12**

BB-076 **"Fuckers of Everything on the Crazy Shitting Planet of the Vomit At smosphere" Mykle Hansen -** Three bizarro satires. Monster Cocks, Journey to the Center of Agnes Cuddlebottom, and Crazy Shitting Planet. **228 pages $12**

BB-077 **"The Kissing Bug" Daniel Scott Buck -** In the tradition of Roald Dahl, Tim Burton, and Edward Gorey, comes this bizarro anti-war children's story about a bohemian conenose kissing bug who falls in love with a human woman. **116 pages $10**

BB-078 **"MachoPoni" Lotus Rose -** It's My Little Pony... *Bizarro* style! A long time ago Poniworld was split in two. On one side of the Jagged Line is the Pastel Kingdom, a magical land of music, parties, and positivity. On the other side of the Jagged Line is Dark Kingdom inhabited by an army of undead ponies. **148 pages $11**

BB-079 **"The Faggiest Vampire" Carlton Mellick III -** A Roald Dahl-esque children's story about two faggy vampires who partake in a mustache competition to find out which one is truly the faggiest. **104 pages $10**

BB-080 **"Sky Tongues" Gina Ranalli -** The autobiography of Sky Tongues, the biracial hermaphrodite actress with tongues for fingers. Follow her strange life story as she rises from freak to fame. **204 pages $12**

BB-081 **"Washer Mouth" Kevin L. Donihe** - A washing machine becomes human and pursues his dream of meeting his favorite soap opera star. **244 pages $11**

BB-082 **"Shatnerquake" Jeff Burk** - All of the characters ever played by William Shatner are suddenly sucked into our world. Their mission: hunt down and destroy the real William Shatner. **100 pages $10**

BB-083 **"The Cannibals of Candyland" Carlton Mellick III** - There exists a race of cannibals that are made of candy. They live in an underground world made out of candy. One man has dedicated his life to killing them all. **170 pages $11**

BB-084 **"Slub Glub in the Weird World of the Weeping Willows"** **Andrew Goldfarb** - The charming tale of a blue glob named Slub Glub who helps the weeping willows whose tears are flooding the earth. There are also hyenas, ghosts, and a voodoo priest **100 pages $10**

BB-085 **"Super Fetus" Adam Pepper** - Try to abort this fetus and he'll kick your ass! **104 pages $10**

BB-086 **"Fistful of Feet" Jordan Krall** - A bizarro tribute to spaghetti westerns, featuring Cthulhu-worshipping Indians, a woman with four feet, a crazed gunman who is obsessed with sucking on candy, Syphilis-ridden mutants, sexually transmitted tattoos, and a house devoted to the freakiest fetishes. **228 pages $12**

BB-087 **"Ass Goblins of Auschwitz" Cameron Pierce** - It's Monty Python meets Nazi exploitation in a surreal nightmare as can only be imagined by Bizarro author Cameron Pierce. **104 pages $10**

BB-088 **"Silent Weapons for Quiet Wars" Cody Goodfellow** - "This is high-end psychological surrealist horror meets bottom-feeding low-life crime in a techno-thrilling science fiction world full of Lovecraft and magic..." -John Skipp **212 pages $12**

BB-089 **"Warrior Wolf Women of the Wasteland" Carlton Mellick III**
Road Warrior Werewolves versus McDonaldland Mutants...post-apocalyptic fiction has never been quite like this. **316 pages $13**

BB-090 **"Cursed" Jeremy C Shipp** - The story of a group of characters who believe they are cursed and attempt to figure out who cursed them and why. A tale of stylish absurdism and suspenseful horror. **218 pages $15**

BB-091 **"Super Giant Monster Time" Jeff Burk** - A tribute to choose your own adventures and Godzilla movies. Will you escape the giant monsters that are rampaging the fuck out of your city and shit? Or will you join the mob of alien-controlled punk rockers causing chaos in the streets? What happens next depends on you. **188 pages $12**

BB-092 **"Perfect Union" Cody Goodfellow** - "Cronenberg's THE FLY on a grand scale: human/insect gene-spliced body horror, where the human hive politics are as shocking as the gore." -John Skipp. **272 pages $13**

BB-093 **"Sunset with a Beard" Carlton Mellick III** - 14 stories of surreal science fiction. **200 pages $12**

BB-094 **"My Fake War" Andersen Prunty** - The absurd tale of an unlikely soldier forced to fight a war that, quite possibly, does not exist. It's Rambo meets Waiting for Godot in this subversive satire of American values and the scope of the human imagination. **128 pages $11**

BB-095**"Lost in Cat Brain Land" Cameron Pierce** - Sad stories from a surreal world. A fascist mustache, the ghost of Franz Kafka, a desert inside a dead cat. Primordial entities mourn the death of their child. The desperate serve tea to mysterious creatures. A hopeless romantic falls in love with a pterodactyl. And much more. **152 pages $11**

BB-096 **"The Kobold Wizard's Dildo of Enlightenment +2" Carlton Mellick III** - A Dungeons and Dragons parody about a group of people who learn they are only made up characters in an AD&D campaign and must find a way to resist their nerdy teenaged players and retarded dungeon master in order to survive. 232 **pages $12**

BB-097 "My Heart Said No, but the Camera Crew Said Yes!" Bradley Sands - A collection of short stories that are crammed with the delightfully odd and the scurrilously silly. **140 pages $13**

BB-098 "A Hundred Horrible Sorrows of Ogner Stump" Andrew Goldfarb - Goldfarb's acclaimed comic series. A magical and weird journey into the horrors of everyday life. **164 pages $11**

BB-099 "Pickled Apocalypse of Pancake Island" Cameron Pierce
A demented fairy tale about a pickle, a pancake, and the apocalypse. **102 pages $8**

BB-100 "Slag Attack" Andersen Prunty - Slag Attack features four visceral, noir stories about the living, crawling apocalypse. A slag is what survivors are calling the slug-like maggots raining from the sky, burrowing inside people, and hollowing out their flesh and their sanity. **148 pages $11**

BB-101 "Slaughterhouse High" Robert Devereaux - A place where schools are built with secret passageways, rebellious teens get zippers installed in their mouths and genitals, and once a year, on that special night, one couple is slaughtered and the bits of their bodies are kept as souvenirs. **304 pages $13**

BB-102 "The Emerald Burrito of Oz" John Skipp & Marc Levinthal
OZ IS REAL! Magic is real! The gate is really in Kansas! And America is finally allowing Earth tourists to visit this weird-ass, mysterious land. But when Gene of Los Angeles heads off for summer vacation in the Emerald City, little does he know that a war is brewing...a war that could destroy both worlds. **280 pages $13**

BB-103 "The Vegan Revolution... with Zombies" David Agranoff
When there's no more meat in hell, the vegans will walk the earth. **160 pages $11**

BB-104 "The Flappy Parts" Kevin L Donihe - Poems about bunnies, LSD, and police abuse. You know, things that matter. 132 **pages $11**

BB-105 **"Sorry I Ruined Your Orgy" Bradley Sands** - Bizarro humorist Bradley Sands returns with one of the strangest, most hilarious collections of the year. **130 pages $11**

BB-106 **"Mr. Magic Realism" Bruce Taylor** - Like Golden Age science fiction comics written by Freud, *Mr. Magic Realism* is a strange, insightful adventure that spans the furthest reaches of the galaxy, exploring the hidden caverns in the hearts and minds of men, women, aliens, and biomechanical cats. **152 pages $11**

BB-107 **"Zombies and Shit" Carlton Mellick III** - "Battle Royale" meets "Return of the Living Dead." Mellick's bizarro tribute to the zombie genre. **308 pages $13**

BB-108 **"The Cannibal's Guide to Ethical Living" Mykle Hansen** - Over a five star French meal of fine wine, organic vegetables and human flesh, a lunatic delivers a witty, chilling, disturbingly sane argument in favor of eating the rich.. **184 pages $11**

  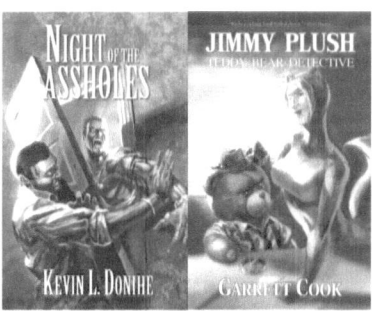

BB-109 **"Starfish Girl" Athena Villaverde** - In a post-apocalyptic underwater dome society, a girl with a starfish growing from her head and an assassin with sea anenome hair are on the run from a gang of mutant fish men. **160 pages $11**

BB-110 **"Lick Your Neighbor" Chris Genoa** - Mutant ninjas, a talking whale, kung fu masters, maniacal pilgrims, and an alcoholic clown populate Chris Genoa's surreal, darkly comical and unnerving reimagining of the first Thanksgiving. **303 pages $13**

BB-111 **"Night of the Assholes" Kevin L. Donihe** - A plague of assholes is infecting the countryside. Normal everyday people are transforming into jerks, snobs, dicks, and douchebags. And they all have only one purpose: to make your life a living hell.. **192 pages $11**

BB-112 **"Jimmy Plush, Teddy Bear Detective" Garrett Cook** - Hardboiled cases of a private detective trapped within a teddy bear body. **180 pages $11**